D1431483

Reluctant Desire

Reluctant Desire

Catherine Grant

ROBERT HALE · LONDON

LAKE PARK PUBLIC LIBRARY

© Catherine Grant 1994
First published in Great Britain 1994

ISBN 0 7090 5493 9

Robert Hale Limited
Clerkenwell House
Clerkenwell Green
London EC1R 0HT

The right of Catherine Grant to be identified as
author of this work has been asserted by her
in accordance with the Copyright, Designs and
Patents Act 1988.

Printed and bound in
Great Britain by
WBC Book Manufacturers Ltd.,
Bridgend, Mid-Glamorgan

One

Lucy Elliot wished she was still in France. But she wasn't. She was here, not that she was sure where *here* was exactly nor that her arrival at this point was particularly decided by her own volition either. Nonetheless, the welcoming image of the small Breton town she had left yesterday lingered, fuelling her irritation into a fresh impatience.

She wondered how far she was from Peter's cottage. His sketchy directions had not prepared her for this. She scowled into the darkness, while the rain pounded down relentlessly and the wind battered the sides of her little Renault, its hazard lights winking distress. Under these conditions any other vehicle approaching her car needed all the advance warning she could muster.

She supposed there was room for blame on her part. But how was she to know that her fuel would not last until the next garage? However she had to reluctantly acknowledge that she had been unprepared to accommodate the scarcity of services. She was aware of the need to replenish the tank, but it had been disconcerting to discover the small filling station in the most recent village she had travelled through was closed. She had been so sure that this road was the final part of the journey up from London.

The route, Peter had explained to her earlier that day while feeding coins into his payphone, led past the private road that went up to Monk Hall, and from where she would be directed, on his assurance, the small distance through the woods to his cottage. Damn Peter for his tactics! Lucy fumed to herself. She need not have come. Why had he not come to London and to her instead? Now she was stranded.

She drummed her fingers on the steering wheel, then switched on the interior light and glanced at her watch because the clock on the dash was faulty. It was a good thirty minutes since she had stopped and it was nearly eleven. Peter would be frantic. Her brows beetled at the thought of him – he had better be feeling frantic. Lucy brightened with optimism as she imagined it. Of course! He was bound to come looking for her – eventually. As if on cue she spotted the lights of a vehicle ahead, high up, somewhere to her right as if coming down a steep track. The Stygian darkness obliterated the Cumbrian landscape. Her eyes followed the beam of headlights and she could pick out the sheeting rain that whipped its horizontal pattern across the moorland and, as it drew closer, she began to hear the drone of its engine. Her eyes picked out the outline of a Range Rover reducing its speed as it finished the steep descent. The bright glare filled the road as it paused before swinging out on to the road towards the car. The headlights dazzled her for a moment, making her blink uncomfortably. She grabbed the door handle and stepped out on to the road.

It roared on, picking up speed. Lucy leaned back into her car and banged on the horn. The blast was short and angry, echoing her emotions. Surely the fool disappearing around the bend could see she was in trouble! Exploding with exasperation, she stared out into the blackness, the rain cascading down her face, hair and neck, and, heedless of the wet or the wind, her hands on her hips, she glared into the night, grinding her teeth at the sound of the vehicle, still picking up speed down the road.

'So much for the kindness of country folk! That driver must be deaf and blind,' she muttered to herself, shaking back the wet tangles of auburn curls away from her face. She licked her lips against the driving rain and began to shiver, clambering back hastily into the dry. In no time a fresh set of lights arced the road, approaching from her rear. She twisted around and stared at them, watching with a glimmer of satisfaction as, whoever it was, drew slowly to a halt behind her. Her eyebrows disappeared into her rain-flattened fringe. It looked awfully like the same Range Rover which had just driven on past a few moments earlier. Her mouth set decisively, she was going to look forward to this.

A man emerged from the driving seat. He was easily visible in the bright twin beams of his headlights – tall, long-legged, casually dressed in blue jeans and leather jacket. He jogged towards her. Lucy did not get out this time but, instead, wound down her window and looked at him, her backbone stiff with indignation.

His voice was cultured and deep. 'What's the problem?'

Sarcasm sharpened her words as she looked up at him. 'I'm in trouble – as you can see—' Unable to stop herself adding, 'I thought you were nearly going to ignore me – ploughing past like that—'

His argument put her smartly in her place. 'I could hardly stop over there and block the entire road especially so near the bend, could I? A pretty recipe for an accident if some clot came tearing up from the village at speed. The inn will be closing shortly and there'll likely be some traffic from it along here soon. Would you have liked that on your conscience?' He looked around him displaying a hard-muscled jaw. 'Nor could you have picked a worse place to get stuck, if I may say so.' She stiffened with dislike at the advantage of his superior knowledge. 'I gather you need some help?'

'Yes.' The word literally hissed out of her mouth as she snapped back with, 'I've run out of fuel.'

His eyes scrutinized her fully. She felt he was enjoying this. 'Really?' She detected his amusement with fresh chagrin. 'You've picked a heck of a night to do that. Jake's will have closed early today, but I expect you wouldn't have known that.'

'Choice had nothing to do with it, although I assume *Jake's* is the station down in the village and I'll readily admit to a lack of knowledge concerning your quaint hours of business in these parts, as I'm only a visitor to the region,' she stated flatly, flicking back her wet curls and noticing without any remorse how drenched he was becoming, although his blouson-styled leather jacket afforded some protection against the elements. His hair was short and thick, framing his well-defined features like a sculptured cap, dark and wet against his head, its colouring obscured by the night and the rain. She caught his thoughtful glance, which made her ask him, rather hastily, 'I'm looking for Monk Hall – is it far?'

She detected the faint pause before he responded. 'No – not far at all. You're expected there?'

'No—' she said without thought, then closed her mouth. Something had altered between them. There was a changed tone in his voice. Surprise, maybe? Interest, she wondered? Definitely. Her scalp lifted, scenting a danger she could not define. Suddenly she realized just how foolish it really was of her to be stranded alone along this isolated road with him. He was a perfect stranger. He looked all right – he looked too good – extremely rugged and attractive. In the full light of the beams she could acknowledge that, yet she had blithely told him enough information to render her a potential victim if his inclination signified a sinister, potentially deadly, intent. Her fingers tightened on the window handle, nerving herself to wind it up quickly, relieved that, out of habit, she had automatically locked her door.

Her head jerked as he said, in a noticeably softened tone, 'It's OK. Don't panic.'

'I'm not panicking,' she answered back quickly, confused now, not daring to wind up the window at this moment, leaving it down, making her vulnerable, so that her heart rate accelerated out of control.

'I'll take you up to Monk Hall, if you like.'

'I don't know—'

'Monk Hall is my home,' he replied swiftly, his hand reaching into the inside pocket of his jacket. 'I can prove it. My name's Mortimer – Joel Mortimer.'

'Oh! Are you? There's no need to prove it. I believe it.' She hoped that she sounded authoritative, or at least, she told herself, in control; her imagination already seeing him withdrawing a concealed weapon of some sort.

He smiled, withdrawing his hand, and to her relief it was empty. 'I wasn't expecting a caller at this time of night. Perhaps you might like to tell me your name and your business here?'

'I'm meeting my—' She realized explaining her presence was rather a waste of time at this particular moment and besides her business was very much her own, and certainly not anything to do with this hard-eyed stranger, so instead supplied only Peter's name. 'Mr Elliot.'

He leaned lower, his breath warming her cheek. 'Elliot!'

'Yes – Peter Elliot – and I'm Lucy Elliot.'

'Oh!' His voice flattened with disappointment.

'Do you know Peter?'

'I know him. Fortunately he's not staying at Monk Hall.'

She ignored the laconic reference. 'Yes, I'm aware of that. He said I'd get directed to his place from the staff at the Hall.'

'You want to go to Rose Cottage?' She thought his expression tightened as she nodded, yet his answers confirmed he was no threat to her, so his next words took her completely by surprise. 'Then he could at least have warned my manager you were coming, couldn't he?'

She was instantly on the defensive, scowling back at him. 'Why should that be necessary?'

He smiled without mirth. 'Even in these remote, backwood places we country folk monitor any strange traffic – especially when it's passing across private land and so, under the circumstances it was, but I don't care to labour the point. How long have you been stranded here?'

Lucy suspected he was making a mocking reference to her 'quaint' remark and did not bother to answer him, expelling her breath in irritation at this tiresome interrogation. The rain poured down relentlessly in a steady, unceasing rhythm. Thankfully the wind buffeted the far side of the car, so leaving her window down did not present the problem of her getting wet. But he was.

A ditch gurgled nearby on the far verge, concealed beneath the bank of ferns, coping with the deluge draining from the steep fell. The man was getting more soaked by the second, yet he preferred to argue with her rather than do something about it. Their eyes clashed again, summoning her reply. 'Look, I've been hanging around here long enough. Peter must be worried – and I've had a heck of a long drive up from London. Have you some spare fuel in a can? Or do you think you could take me up there?'

'Oh, I thought I'd already made that offer.'

'Oh really, Mr Mortimer, must you make an issue out of this?'

His voice was gentle. 'I rather think you initiated the issue.'

'I did not!'

'Didn't you?'

She held her breath, her senses on full alert at the current flowing between them which led her finally to stammer out in confusion, 'Do – do you like quarrelling just for the sake of it in this pouring rain?'

'Was I doing that?' He straightened and stood back. 'Then I do apologize – come on – let's get up there. My fuel can's empty. Lock up and give me your keys. I'll arrange to have someone come down to fill your tank and bring your car up to Rose Cottage.'

He was calm and collected as he moved off. The current dissipated and Lucy blushed in the shadowed confines of her car at the fanciful notions which had just crossed her thoughts. What had just happened must have been a product of her imagination. She felt riddled with shame and followed him meekly, grabbing her canvas holdall from the back seat before locking up the Renault. He was waiting for her, standing by the passenger side of his Range Rover. He took the holdall from her and threw it in the back. Her high heels caught her out and she stumbled into her seat, banging her kneecap in the process as she encountered a hard, metal box stacked on the floor, cursing softly, uncomfortably aware that her slender, bare limbs were damp beneath her short swing-style skirt. Her car keys slid from her numb fingers and dropped on to the floor beneath her seat.

'Damn and blast!' she muttered, groping around to retrieve them, aware that her skirt had hitched up to an alarming angle around her thigh. She found the keys after a few moments, aware that he was waiting for her to settle safely in her seat. She clutched them in one hand while she smoothed down the hem of her skirt with her other hand then hugged her fine woollen blazer more tightly around her, more chilled than she realized, shivering a little in the cool night air. The sharp wind lifted the hem of her skirt and revealed another fresh expanse of thigh before her driver closed her door and walked around to the driver's seat. The current became vibrantly alive again, making her spine stiffen with the shock of it as soon as he climbed in beside her. She attempted to counter that wayward imagination of hers with the explanation that it stemmed from the events of the night, the hectic phone call from Peter, the turbulence of her thoughts as she travelled north, the frustrations encountered at the end of her journey ... she blushed and shuffled her legs tightly together.

'It's really very kind of you to help me out,' she started to say as he indicated and swung slowly out past her car and turned up the road from which he had so recently driven down.

'It's the least I could do.'

She raised an eyebrow in the darkness and firmed her mouth, her fingers playing with her car keys. The man was unpredictable: scowling one moment yet charming the next. She hoped the ride would be short as she sunk back against her seat as the road steepened and twisted. He drove slowly; sheep grazed, heedless of the elements, by the side of the road, and now and again he had to stop while some of them ran blindly across in front of his path.

Presently the road levelled out, and they were moving through a forest of tall firs. Her driver opened his window a little. She could smell the full, fresh scent filling the vehicle. A small animal scuttled across the road in front of them.

'Oh look!' she cried out with surprise and pleasure.

'A stoat,' he explained, and she caught his eye and saw his mouth curving with amusement. Instead of a mature twenty-four he made her feel suddenly sixteen again.

Reluctant Desire

They emerged from the forest and Lucy saw Monk Hall. It looked large and imposing; thin chimneys speared the sky and the gaunt, grey-stoned walls were offset by Georgian-styled windows; a walled courtyard enclosed the whole residence, with a wide archway to the left. They drove straight beneath the archway and emerged into a neatly cobbled square courtyard. In the centre was a grassed area on which stood an ancient bricked well. A neat range of smaller outbuildings surrounded them, most in darkness, but overhead a sophisticated exterior lighting system spilled across them. The Range Rover stopped near the rear of the house itself.

The rain had blessedly ceased, she noted, not wishing a fresh drenching. The cobbles gleamed brightly, slick and wet. Somewhere, from nearby outhouses, she could hear the sound of dogs barking fiercely. She thought she heard the sound of a horse's whinny through one of the closed stable doors, but could not be sure; the wind still buffeted the tall firs and the dogs made an incredible racket. Her driver ignored them and instead got out and came around to her side, opening her door. She clambered out without help, but her heel caught fast in the cobbles, and she was forced to twist awkwardly to release it, which instead made her nearly stumble.

He was already there. Prepared. His arms held her steady. She was not petite, but he towered over her. His arms were strong and firm, and held her with purpose, not coy or hesitant. His masculinity vibrated through her. She could smell his masculine scent, evoking an instant response that was not unpleasant. 'I'm sorry,' she murmured against his chest and she noticed he was quick to release her, his action a rejection in itself. The leather of his jacket was streaked with rain, it left damp patches against the thin fabric of her blazer. Lucy looked up at him but his face was turned away from the light. She was unable to read the expression in his eyes; dark eyes, she noticed.

'Come inside. Winnie will give you a hot drink while I arrange things.'

'Thanks.' She followed him through a back door. 'Would you mind if I telephone Peter? He must be worried—'

Joel Mortimer swung around and faced her. Not all the lighting in the kitchen was switched on, but where he stood a spotlight spilled revealingly across his face. She could see his eyes now very clearly in its light. Dark-blue eyes, jewel bright, framed by dark lashes, and his hair was light-coloured, pale brown, almost fair, she guessed, when dry. His face was angular, strongly shaped, with a determined chin that showed, at this late hour the beginnings of a faint stubble. His mouth twisted, a sensual mouth, full and firm and his smile was cold. 'I'm sorry, I can't do that. The cottage has no telephone.'

'Oh!' She recalled Peter's telephone conversation with her earlier. He had used a coin-operated machine. 'My mistake, Mr Mortimer.'

'The name's Joel.'

'Joel.' It sounded good on her tongue as she said it. 'Thanks anyway.'

'I'll take you over in a few minutes – there's plenty of time. I expect my tenant hasn't left the pub in the village yet. *Winnie*,' he called out, while opening a door that led into a darkened passageway. There was silence. He closed the door and glanced at his wristwatch, muttering abstractedly, 'She's probably left for home by now. I expect Andrew came down for her.'

'It doesn't matter. If you'll just show me—'

'I think not. Come on, I need a hot drink to warm myself up, besides—' He stopped, busying himself to fill the kettle and plant it on to the hob of an Aga.

'Besides what?' she prompted, glancing around the gleaming modern fitments of the kitchen in this vastly proportioned room with its low slung beams crossing the length of the ceiling. Bright copper pots hung on great hooks suspended from the beams overhead a large, scrubbed table which dominated the centre of the room but, because of the partial lighting and the heat radiating from the Aga, the room was thrown into a haven of warmth and intimacy.

His eyes met hers, ignoring the question, or evading it, she could not be sure when he asked instead, 'Sure I couldn't tempt you into taking a tea, coffee or something else? Perhaps you might prefer a hot chocolate?'

'A hot chocolate sounds terrific,' she grinned. He smiled back, reaching into a cupboard to prepare her drink, and Lucy felt her stomach turn to liquid.

Something caught his attention and within a few seconds she heard it too for his dogs were barking again. The man straightened from the cupboard, setting down the mugs. 'Someone's coming up – I'll check.'

He strode out of the kitchen, leaving her watching a boiling kettle. The dogs were setting up quite another racket by now. She could hear a car enter the courtyard. From inside the house she could detect the screech of erratic braking, she recognized that immediately. Peter. Her lips formed his name soundlessly.

She hastened towards the back door. The owner of Monk Hall returned, bringing with him a louder more excited cacophony of dog barking which refused to cease. Then Peter appeared behind him. Lucy relaxed with relief. His tall, lean figure emerged behind the slightly taller figure of his landlord, but there was the same endearingly familiar, light-blond hair swept in a fashionably short style that brushed away in wet slicks from his thin face, his sharp rain-swept features registering a mixture of irritation and concern which made her smile widen with pleasure. He was nearly as tall as Joel Mortimer, but not quite and nowhere near as broad or muscular, although Peter was a good six feet in height. It made Joel Mortimer look a mountain of a man beside him, she noted, irritated with herself that she should be so acutely aware of the stranger. Peter's smile of relief was a welcome respite.

'I ran out of fuel, would you believe it?' was all she could manage to cry while he pushed past Joel, his arms wide and gathered her into him.

The transatlantic accent he had adopted was more noticeable now than on the telephone. It reminded her of the years they had been apart, but his words reassured her that he was still the familiar brother she knew. 'I might have known – scatterbrained – as ever!'

She hugged him wildly, aware of the long period they had been apart from each other. 'Oh! It's so good to see you again, Peter.' And she meant it.

She hugged and kissed him loudly on both cheeks. 'It's been too long,' she added breathlessly.

'Lucy, I know.' Peter set her away from him. 'Your car down the road made me go spare. I thought something had happened to you, for God's sake.'

'She's already explained that she ran out of petrol,' Joel Mortimer put in dryly, observing the scene with a dark air of censure, Lucy detected.

Peter did not notice, his eyes alive with amusement. 'Isn't that typical, my little hare-brained—'

Her rescuer cut in abruptly. 'Look! If you don't mind, it's rather late, and now that you've rediscovered one another—' His face looked set with impatience.

Lucy stared at him, his mood change confused her. 'You're quite right – it is late.' His glance unnerved her. The kettle steamed to the boil on the stove. Joel made no move to make any drinks. Lucy's hands slipped from Peter's shoulders and she moved towards the door. 'As Joel has said – it's getting late. Thanks for bringing me up – all the same.'

Joel Mortimer shrugged away the thanks. 'It was nothing. After all I just happened to be passing the road and saw your hazard lights. I would have been a blind man not to have stopped and helped.' He made it sound so banal and matter of fact. Did he not recall her banging on her horn to alert him? His eyes clashed with hers. 'Manny will have it up in no time.' He extended his hand, 'Give me your keys.'

'Manny?'

'His manager,' Peter supplied crisply, instantly

alert to coolness invading the other man's expression.

She placed them on the table. 'Thanks – awfully. I'm most grateful and sorry that I—'

'Don't be.'

'Come on, Lucy,' Peter urged, 'my car's outside, let's get home.'

Joel followed them outside and, ignoring Peter, said, 'You'll have your car outside Rose Cottage early next morning – if that's convenient – Lucy.'

'Thanks a lot, Joel.'

'I assume you are staying there' – he kept his voice light – 'for long?'

Peter's voice was rough. 'Of course she's staying there! Why shouldn't she?' Lucy swallowed hard at the belligerence exchanged by the men.

'As the owner of the cottage and as you're my tenant – if you study the terms of your agreement it clearly states that I have the right to be firstly informed. So it's very much my business.'

'Oh well!' Peter's mouth snapped shut. He thrust his hands into his cord pants and Lucy saw the distinct swagger in his figure as he looked sullenly at his landlord.

Lucy tried to smooth the difficult moment. 'I don't think Peter was aware of his obligations.'

'It seems not.'

'And he is now, and so am I.'

'You're not at fault.'

Lucy interrupted Joel's startled apology. 'He – he wasn't sure if I was coming up, you see.'

'It's really none of my business—'

'Look, it's three years since we last saw each other,' Lucy felt obliged to explain, taken aback at the fresh hostility between the men. 'Is that a problem?' she asked him bluntly, her light-grey eyes fastened upon Joel Mortimer's brooding face.

He looked untouched. 'No – of course not. Stay on as long as you wish. I'll inform Manny accordingly.'

Peter scowled, his dark-brown eyes gleaming like gimlets in the gloom of the kitchen. 'As long as she wishes!' he snorted. 'That's interesting! Considering that I got the distinct impression I wasn't extended that kind of hospitality.'

'Whatever gave you that idea, Elliot?'

Peter scowled back at him. 'You know damn well what!'

'You brought that situation upon yourself if you remember.'

'You can stuff your preconceived judgement!' Peter growled back.

'Peter!' Lucy wailed, wringing her hands. 'What is all this about?'

Her voice changed it immediately. They both looked at her. Joel Mortimer's eyes flashed angrily for a brief moment, but not at Lucy, as he told her, 'I'm sorry, this argument is rather pointless – under the circumstances. If you wish to move on to Rose Cottage, I suggest you make a start. It is getting rather late, and it remains a priority that your car has to be removed from the road below, so if you don't mind I have some business to attend to on your behalf.'

Lucy would have liked Peter to have stepped in and taken charge of removing her car, but the strong smell of alcohol on his breath stopped her thinking about it, and besides, she doubted he had a spare can of petrol to oversee the matter. It rattled her that she had to stand there and say nothing. There was not really anything she could do. Joel Mortimer had the upper hand, in every way.

'Come on, Lucy,' said Peter, grabbing her arm.

She propped him up and extended the palm of one hand. 'Give me your car keys. I'll drive.'

Peter grinned sheepishly, searching in the front of his jeans' pocket, and withdrew a bunch of keys.

'You'll need your bag.' Joel moved out ahead of them to retrieve her holdall from his Range Rover. The wind had dropped and it had begun to drizzle. Joel did not linger while he transferred her baggage to Peter's sports car. His dogs barked furiously from beyond the barn doors. No one spoke. Lucy climbed into the ancient MG, oblivious to the set atmosphere, shivering openly in the cool air and settling down on to a very damp, leather-clad seat. The hood was strapped back and she had no intention of attempting to put it up at this late stage. Peter climbed in beside her. The dogs barked, then howled, whining plaintively as he snapped his door shut and glared up at his landlord.

By now Lucy was annoyed with them both at their mysterious behaviour. She switched on the engine and, putting it into gear, started forward, rather jerkily, much to her annoyance. She could see a clear track outside the courtyard and Peter pointed down the hill, which looked like the opposite side of the fell from where she had travelled up with Joel Mortimer. Temper made her incautious and she drove Peter's precious collector's dream of a model rather jerkily down an unmade-up track. Joel did not stop to watch them, she noticed in the rear-view mirror, seeing how impatiently he made for his house, almost as if he was glad to see the back of them. It did not enhance her mood or her driving technique.

'Steady on,' Peter said, grabbing at the wheel when she nearly took them into the hedge. Fumes of alcohol overwhelmed her almost as his breath hit her cheek. 'Take care—'

It was a few minutes' drive; the wipers cleared the dirty windscreen and Lucy peered out into unfamiliar territory. Trees, hillocks, a flock of sheep passed her way – the descent of the track seemed endless, twisting, turning, bumpy. A light appeared out of nowhere as she took a steep bend and there it was, the cottage, nestled snugly against a thick outcrop of firs. A porchlight spilled out into he roadway and Lucy pulled up to a stop outside.

'There's something I'd better tell you – before we go in.'

'Oh yes.' She peered at the open garage doors adjacent to the old cottage. 'Should I take her in there?'

'Who?' Peter stared at her rather stupidly.

She glared back at him. 'Your car, idiot!'

'Oh! Yes, of course.'

She put it into gear, and then the door of the cottage opened, and a slender figure appeared in the welcoming glow of the doorway. A young girl, small with long dark hair, hovered on the step.

She took Lucy completely by surprise. 'Who on earth's that?' she asked as she allowed the car to ease forward into the darkened opening of the garage.

'My daughter, Sophia,' he admitted, and Lucy's exclamation of surprise was clearly audible to the child as the MG screeched to a sudden halt within inches of meeting the garage wall.

Two.

'Daughter!' Lucy cried. 'No wonder you were so evasive on the phone.'

Peter had more important items on his mind. 'Do you realize you nearly crashed my car! Have you any idea of its worth?'

Lucy knew his priorities. 'You're not even married – and besides, I expect the car's insured.'

'That's not a particularly necessary criterion these days.'

'Insurance?' Lucy queried blankly.

'Marriage.'

Her brother just stared at her in the gloom of the old barn that served as the cottage garage. There were dark rings underneath his eyes, the look of a man not at ease with his life. His next words were more convincing to her as he climbed out of the car. 'I've been ringing your flat number all week. I rang the offices of that French magazine place and they told me you'd finished your contract and were taking a vacation. I knew you'd have to turn up at your flat sometime.'

Lucy got out of the car too. 'Lucky for you I got back this morning. I can't take this in – a daughter! What's her name?'

'Sophia.'

'Oh!' Lucy was suddenly diverted. 'That's a pretty name.'

'Her mother was Italian.'

'Was?'

'She's dead. She developed a tumour – I'm told it was terribly swift. It was her solicitor who got in touch with me.'

'Oh! How sad! You should have told me about them – why didn't you?'

'There's very little to tell – apart from Sophia's existence – and if Maria had not died so suddenly the arrangement I had with her would have remained. We barely kept contact throughout the years. She had her life and I had mine. Sophia was the only thing that kept us in *comunicado*. I never met my child until recently. I thought it better that way. Now, I'm not so sure: she's so adorable, Lucy. Anyway her mother and I had a brief affair when I worked on that project near Florence and that was the end of it – or should have been. I was twenty-three, fresh out of university. Maria was older, thirtyish. I was smitten and so was she. I thought we were enjoying a very adult relationship. Sophia was our major lapse from reason, and we were both stunned that it had happened. I didn't want marriage – nor did she. After that Sophia's mother and I barely communicated – unless there was an urgent need for my financial resources which I duly accepted. Maria obtained a teaching post in England about a year after the child was born. She severed the few family ties in Italy she had and settled in London. After a succession of nannies, Sophia was sent on to boarding-school. Maria accepted my offer to pay the fees. Now *I* have to fulfil my parental role.'

'But why didn't you tell me about them? I wasn't that remote—'

'Weren't you?' His eyes were brilliant with challenge, and she had to look away.

It was not exactly the sort of reaction she was expecting, as she followed him out of the garage, retrieving her holdall herself as she walked behind him towards the cottage. Suddenly she realized three years apart meant a great gap in her own relationship with him. Their parents had died in a road accident when Peter was only thirteen. They were brought up by their mother's parents. Their grandfather was strict, too strict for Peter, which was why, as soon as he could be independent of them, he had left the family home.

Lucy had been more adaptable. She had been adopted as a baby, and although Peter knew the truth of her birth, readily accepting and loving her as his own natural born sister, she had not been told the truth about her parentage by her grandparents until she was in her teens. He was ten years older, and he had left home at nineteen, during his university years. After obtaining his degree he had settled in London, leasing an apartment, while his work as a chemical engineer for a major American company had taken him to all parts of the world. Now he was thirty-four – and the last time she had seen him had been on her twenty-first birthday – three years ago. He had wanted her to come with him to the States and she had bluntly refused. Peter had been terribly hurt; he had wanted to take her under his wing and become responsible for her, almost like a parent, and was totally amazed and unable to understand why she should turn down the chance to continue further studies at an American university, but she had already been offered a post on a regional magazine which she had happily accepted. He could not come to terms with her desire to have her own freedom to choose how to live, even if she had acquired the inclination through the family, particularly through his influence, rather than by the genetics of her own birthright. Last year, when she had been given the opportunity of promotion to fashion editor on a major European magazine she had wired him her news and Peter had not responded, much to her disappointment. His ambitions had never embraced hers.

The child was standing where she had first spotted her, waiting for them. Her bare toes peeped beneath the hem of a white cotton nightdress between the opened folds of a pale-green dressing-gown. Lucy's heart melted at the sight of her – Peter's flesh and blood. That made her an *aunt*. She felt light-headed.

'Sophia, love, get inside,' she heard him tell the child as they approached the cottage. Her pulse leapt at the inflexion in her brother's voice. He was not unaffected by his daughter, whatever the circumstances.

'Papa—'

Lucy felt the tears sting her eyes. One word: *Papa* – she was already overcome.

'Is this your girlfriend?' The small voice quavered with unshed tears, Lucy could tell. She felt suddenly protective and aware of the vulnerability of the young child. The child stepped indoors as they hurried inside. Lucy closed the door, enjoying the welcome heat of a coal fire burning brightly from beyond the wire fireguard protecting the stone hearth. It was a comfortable room, a large chesterfield dominated one wall, and there were two, deeply sprung armchairs at either side of the hearth. The television set was switched on. A forties-style black and white movie was playing on the screen, the sound switched down. She must have done that when she had heard the car coming down the bank, Lucy thought. She must have been waiting for him. She fixed her attention on Peter's daughter. Her brother was right. Dark haired she might be, but she had Peter's brown eyes, and square chin and that same large determined mouth.

'This is your aunt,' her father stated, 'and she's come to stay with us for a little while. She's your Aunt Lucy.'

The child blinked solemnly at Lucy and then turned to Peter with more urgent considerations on her young mind than meeting a strange relation. 'I was frightened, Papa.'

'Frightened? What of?'

'I heard an owl outside, in the tall trees. It called out. I woke up in my bed and heard it calling out. It was calling to me – up there in the tall trees that nearly hit my window. It terrified me.'

'It wouldn't have been calling to you, silly, it was after its supper, I dare say.'

The big dark eyes looked at him, diverted, suddenly accusing. 'I didn't have any. The fridge is empty. It's always empty.'

'I left you some potato crisps and a box of chocolates. I thought that's what you kids eat when the grown-ups go out.'

'Peter, really!' Her brother's name slipped from Lucy's lips with censure.

The child still ignored her. The long, shining hair tossed in a flounce across her shoulders as she stared back at her father, challenging him, 'So! You were away hours and hours. You said you would be back by ten – I watched the clock – you never came. The owl hooted and I became terrified. I might as well have stopped at school throughout this vacation – I would have had more attention – and I wouldn't have been so afraid.'

'I only went out at—'

'It was ages ago.'

'Was it, poppet?' Lucy stared at them both. Peter had charm – more than his fair share. Sophia was not immune. He grinned at his daughter, a lopsided grin, his eyes full of shame. 'I'm a lousy papa, aren't I? Whatever can I do to make up for it, eh?'

'No, no—' Sophia denied, her voice very small. 'Never that.' Her eyes filled with tears. 'I was just frightened – here on my own.' Her small chin wobbled. 'If Mr Mortimer hadn't arrived I—' Her eyes flashed with eloquence. 'He was very angry with you when he called.'

'Oh great!' Peter snarled back, the endearing grin wiped cleanly from his face. His daughter's face crumpled with the threat of tears at the savagery in his tone. 'Just when did he call, might I ask?'

'Ear-earlier,' the child stammered. 'I forget the time. He checked the fire for me, it was nearly out – he built it up into warm flames again and I soon forgot how cold I was when I—' The child bit her lip and looked at the rug on the floor, before going on. 'Then he put up the guard which you had forgotten about. He told me a funny story about an owl. It made me laugh.' She giggled brokenly, thinking about it, and immediately the tears that threatened disappeared.

Lucy glanced at the fire and frowned, but said nothing, but she had a good idea just where Joel Mortimer was heading for when he stopped to rescue her, she stared at Peter and he could not mistake the disapproval that crossed her small features.

'Look, Lucy, a man has got to have some space. I only drove down for a couple of pints and a chat for half an hour with the locals. I aimed to be on the road back long before you arrived. But there was a darts match and I got involved. It was fun and, well, we were winning for goodness sake. I couldn't very well abandon my team, now could I? I guess I lost track of the time. Anyway, I left Sophia tucked up in bed. She was fast asleep when I drove down to the village.' He glared back at his daughter. 'Or so I thought.'

Lucy sighed. 'That's not really good enough, and you should have the intelligence to admit it.'

Sophia looked on with real distress. 'I really was asleep, Papa. The owl woke me up – that's why I was frightened. It startled me.'

Peter's lips thinned. 'And Mortimer walked in – just like that.'

Sophia's wonderful long hair shook with indignation as she moved her head. 'No – by then I was outside—'

'Outdoors!' Her father was outraged. 'Outside the cottage! Out in the open! In the middle of the night – and the pouring rain! Doing what?'

'I thought I'd look in the barn and see if your car was there – I thought you might be outside, maybe

– I wasn't sure. I was just looking for you. Mr Mortimer drove by and saw me. He thought I was in trouble. I suppose I was, at the time.'

'You'll be in deeper trouble if I catch you wandering out alone in the dark at the dead of night again.'

'I'm sorry, Papa.'

'It wasn't your fault, Sophia,' Lucy stated gently, setting down her bag and shrugging out of her wet jacket. 'Take me to the kitchen and I'll rustle us some hot milk maybe – or perhaps you'd like something else? I'll see what I can find, hmm?'

For the first time the child smiled at her with genuine gratitude in her wide eyes. 'Thank you, very much. Do I have to call you Aunt? You look too young – you're more like the sixth formers at my school almost!'

'Then plain Lucy will suffice, don't you think?' her aunt prompted, warmed by the wide smile that cleared Sophia's face and vanished the heaviness that laced her young brow.

Despite what had happened, Lucy slept well in the tiny bedroom upstairs. She opened her eyes, scanning the strange room, with its dormer window that faced the east, and settled back on the narrow bed while her mind struggled to absorb the revelations of the previous night. She lay for some time, deep in thought.

The sound of the motor diverted her, she recognized the engine of her own Renault and slid reluctantly from the bedcovers, her bare toes curling on the polished wood floor as she padded over to the window and threw back the thin cotton curtains patterned with white daisies on a blue background. Through the small panes of glass the view robbed her momentarily of breath. Her grey eyes widened with pleasure at the panorama of steeply sloping fells that met the valley below. She could clearly make out the thin, winding line of the road where she had run out of fuel, and to the left, down below, nestled the village. From beyond the valley where the road ran, the fells dramatically swept upwards again, a broad expanse of moorland, of craggy outcrops, and scabrous clumps of verdant undergrowth that contrasted against the bleakness. Now and then, the swollen rivulets, draining down mountainous crevasses, spilling last night's rainfall, resulted in a scurry of tiny waterfalls, from which, haphazardly, rich bursts of foliage jutted; ferns that were big enough to conceal a sheep, she realized, as she spotted livestock ranging the vast expanse while they grazed. She lifted her eyes to admire the wide expanse of pearl-grey, unsettled sky through which the morning sun thrust its rays in the broken cloud. A car door banged shut. She hurriedly dropped her gaze and met Joel Mortimer's cold eyes, staring up at her.

'Oh!' She clutched the baggy T-shirt against her body and let the curtain fall back to conceal her from him. 'Damn!' Lucy moved back to the safety of the narrow bed and reached for her holdall. Hastily she pulled off her choice of sleep attire and dipped into her bag for something suitable.

'Hello?' His voice rang out in the clear air. She froze like a statue and then pulled the T-shirt back on and returned to the window.

'Give me a moment,' she yelled, after opening the window, her hair a mess of tangles across her cheeks, when she bent her head.

'I'd appreciate a lift back – er – when you're decently ready, of course.'

She caught the humour in his tone and smiled back. 'Yes,' she stammered, unconsciously attempting to pull her hair back from her face, 'of course.'

The movement caused the hem of the shirt to lift above the curve of her buttocks. Her face flamed, even though she knew he could not possibly see anything revealing. Self-consciously she yanked the hem of it down over one buttock and kept it there for a moment. Leaving the window open she quickly withdrew and dressed haphazardly, omitting her bra to save seconds, pulling on a pair of lacy panties then covering her long legs in soft jade leggings, over which she threw on another T-shirt, boldly emblazoned with embroidered slogans advertising a famous aperitif. She thrust her bare feet into her Reebok boots and, lifting the old latch on her door, peered out into the corridor. All was quiet. Peter's door was firmly shut, and so was Sophia's. She hurried downstairs, trying not to make a noise, glancing at the cold uninviting embers in the grate as she hurried towards the front door.

'Good morning.' She was breathless again. Facing him in the daylight, she felt suddenly shy. The cool air made her hug herself as she shivered slightly in the open, her body still warmed from her bed and adjusting to the change of temperature. His gaze was lazy, noting everything, even the way she sucked in her cheeks to warm herself up again.

'Manny brought your car up last night but left it up at the yard. There didn't seem any point in moving it down here until this morning.'

'No, of course not – er, I'm grateful.'

His eyes studied her, openly, and she felt extremely conscious of her bare, unwashed face, and her thick tangle of uncombed hair. His eyes lingered on it. 'It looks like I'm a bit too early—'

'It doesn't matter.' His eyes were the colour of deep sapphire; against the weathered look of his skin they were a startling contrast. His hair was now dry, shining with health, almost a golden-brown, a pale chestnut, she amended, liking the way it thickly moulded his strong-shaped head, yet tidily short which enhanced the rugged outdoors look of his image. This morning he was dressed in a thick beige sweater over a wine-coloured shirt and dark-grey corded pants, his feet thrust into a pair of well-made brogues. He looked crisp and clean, his face closely-shaved.

Lucy shuffled her feet uncomfortably, wriggling her toes beneath the soft leather Reeboks, acutely aware of her scruffy appearance. Yet he didn't seem to find it offensive. In fact his eyes didn't say that at all. She felt her chest tighten, as if she found breathing rather difficult to manage and swallowed harshly, finding her throat dry, and wondered if she might have caught a chill from last night's soaking, coughing experimentally.

'Was everything fine – when he got you here last night?'

Lucy's head shot up. 'What?' she managed on a croak.

'I expect you were warned that I'd called by and found the child.' His lips thinned with disapproval.

'Oh! Yes. Sophia mentioned it.' She crossed her arms in front of her chest, not wishing to be disloyal to Peter, although she knew his landlord had every right to show it. Instead she settled for an appreciative gesture that Sophia's distress had been checked. 'Thanks for calling though, all the same. It really was very kind of you – and – it settled Sophia.'

He misinterpreted it for a dismissal. 'Well, I suppose I should go – would you mind running me back up to the Hall?'

She uncrossed her arms. ' Oh, I hope you didn't think—'

His eyes were very blue. 'Think what?'

'I meant that I'm pleased you checked last night. Sophia likes you.'

'She has a good nerve – for one so young – how old is she?'

'She's ten years old.'

'Ten!'

Lucy shrugged. 'I know, she looks younger; I guess she's small for her age, I suppose.' She was instantly reminded of Peter's description of Maria, Sophie's petite mother, when they had talked in earnest last night, after his daughter had finally been put to bed.

Joel Mortimer thrust his hands into the pockets of his cords. 'I'm sorry that I didn't bring you straight here last night – but I wasn't certain who you were – and I knew the child was alone waiting for her father to return from the inn. She let me know about that.'

She grimaced, not wanting to be reminded of the child – left alone, abandoned for empty, adult pleasure, and instead sighed, knowing there was no way she could make excuses where none could be made. 'I know. I worked that out for myself.'

His thoughts were preoccupied. 'You mentioned that you hadn't seen each other for three years.'

'Yes. That's right – we decided to go our own ways. I've been working in France, and Peter was overseas involved with *his* job – so—'

'And your work?' She glanced up, his eyes seemed fascinated by the colour of her hair. 'What are you heavily involved with? Or should I say were – until you arrived here?'

'I work freelance now. I'm a fashion journalist.'

'Fashion!' His eyebrows jiggled, while he scanned her casual wear, commenting bluntly, 'I'm afraid I'm no expert in that department.' His gaze told her that he thought she was no advert either, which, in her hastily applied clothes, she had to agree with him, and it made her uncomfortable so that she fidgeted with nervousness.

Lucy plucked at her T-shirt, straightening it down her curves, only to define the softening outline of her breasts more clearly. His eyes gleamed with a frankly male satisfaction that caught her unawares. She blushed, feeling the heat prickle her scalp and wished she had taken the time to wear a bra while dressing.

'The child – Sophia isn't it? She tells me she stays at boarding-school in Sussex.'

'That's correct.'

'She's adorable.'

'I'm glad you think so – so do I.'

'And her father? Does he adore her too?'

'But, of course – Why? Can't you tell—'

'Not when he leaves her alone like he did last night – and not on other nights while he's leasing my cottage.'

'Look, I know it doesn't look good but I can explain—'

'I'd be very interested.'

Lucy stared at him, the protective family instinct in her rising, provoked, to the bait. 'But then, I really don't see why it's any of your business, Mr Mortimer, do you?'

His argument was blunt. 'I had no option but to make it mine last night.'

'That was different – there were extenuating circumstances. Besides, Sophia explained why she had run out of the cottage.'

'There was a great deal to explain,' he countered with heat, 'she was absolutely terrified.'

Lucy closed her mouth and stared at him, stiffening. His eyes were cold, almost hostile, she thought, as if he blamed her too. He had not heard what Peter had told her last night; there were definitely unusual circumstances, and Peter was finding it difficult adjusting to his immediate responsibilities of parenthood. She could not deny that, not after last night. What right had this man to pronounce judgement over something about which he knew nothing? His arrogance was more than provoking. She felt an anger harden her insides.

'Perhaps I'd better take you back up to the Hall, as you've requested, Mr Mortimer. I don't want to keep you from your – work, do I? Especially after all the trouble you've gone to on our behalf.'

'Perhaps you're right.'

'I know I am – and can I reassure you that while I am here, Sophia will never be left on her own in that cottage again. Understand?' She gazed behind her. 'I don't want to disturb them – so can we—?'

He glanced up at the dormer window. 'I notice you chose the dormer room – it's very tiny, isn't it?'

She stared at him, watching the darkness invade

his cheeks and answered softly, 'Your cottage is rather lovely, and I liked the little room on the front – if you're probing?'

'Was I?'

She made him follow her to her car, climbing into it, while she started the engine, all done in tense silence. The road – if it could be called that – was awkward; more a lane, a rough, makeshift lane, and the ground was rutted and slippery after the heavy rain. The rear of the Renault protested, moving awkwardly, the wheels spinning a little as she began to make the turn. Her hands slipped on the wheel, and she caught her lower lip anxiously as she glanced in the wing mirror and noticed how she had nearly edged it into the corner of the barn, missing the stone wall with only inches to spare. She could feel her anger milling with humiliation, and bit her lip painfully, alarmed that she could feel as out of control as her car.

'Steady!' His hands caught the wheel, turning it deftly, while he glanced back to correct her steering.

She was overwhelmed with rage. 'Get off!'

'Sorry! I was only trying to help.'

'An assistance I can do without,' she managed in a trite voice.

'It doesn't look that way to me,' he muttered darkly.

The Renault slew round once again, this time wider from the edge of the barn, and without saying another word, although she cursed unhealthily in thought as the gears jammed noisily, she gritted her teeth before she had the car righted and headed, albeit bumpily, up the lane that led on to the more stable track that brought them round to the Hall.

He was gracious enough not to make comment,

she noted, her face flaming, heated with the anger still fermenting inside her, although she could not justly rationalize why she should feel such antipathy towards him. She quelled the argument about how he had rescued her from the lonely road down in the valley the night before. With hindsight, it was perfectly obvious that Peter would have chanced upon her only minutes later, so it would not have been such a disaster waiting a few more minutes, surely? Perhaps she would have been better off waiting that extra time. Unfortunately it was her ill chance that Joel Mortimer happened to be coming down the fell just then, prompted she realized with fresh irritation because of the hapless Sophia, deserted in the cottage.

His cottage.

She drove directly across the cobbled yard and halted the car outside the same door he had taken her to last night. A plump, elderly woman wrapped in a voluminous pink cotton overall immediately appeared at the open doorway.

He broke the silence. 'That's Winnie, she looks after me now and again.'

Her mood was heavy, and Lucy's retort was waspish. 'I would have thought you were the last person who needed looking after, Mr Mortimer. You seem so in control all of the time.' She hated herself, regretting the words as soon as she had uttered them. What was it about this man that made her so irritable? And why did she have to take leave of her senses to say something so stupid?

Three

'I'm sorry,' she told him abruptly, annoyed with herself. 'It was inexcusable of me – please forget what I said.'

However, he evidently did not want to forget, as he asked sharply, 'Is that how you see me?'

'I – I don't know you at all! Why, we only met last night!' she prevaricated.

'It seems it was long enough for you to form an opinion,' he stated flatly.

'Really, Mr Mortimer.' A movement caught Lucy's attention a few yards away; the plump-figured woman watched them keenly, not making any attempt to hurry back indoors.

Her passenger was not diverted; instead his voice softly reminded her with his name. 'Last night it was Joel – remember?'

'Of course. I've been rather ungracious—' Her voice tailed off and his silence made her feel worse. She was strongly aware of him, like last night, his scent filled the space between them, the faint musk scent of a man, mingled with the clean tang of the soap he must have used in his shower that morning. A picture of him under the spray filled her mind and she jolted herself mentally out of it, banishing the image of a strong, muscular body, yet unable to look him in the face for at that moment she knew she would blush. Joel Mortimer was a very astute man; she knew enough about him already to confirm that.

She fixed perplexed eyes on the woman, who was looking at them now, much more curiously this time and smiled nervously at her. The woman did not return the gesture, if anything she looked a little more intrigued.

'If your family are still not up yet, why don't you join me for breakfast?' he suggested more lightly to which she shook her head with vigour, still unable to look at him, the tangle of rich curls swinging against her cheeks. 'Then coffee,' he amended. 'You've time for a coffee, surely?'

He was persistent, she gave him that, the housekeeper's brow beetled, it made Lucy relent. 'I suppose so.'

Lucy walked with him, a little self-consciously. She expected to be led into the kitchen, where he had taken her last night, but he ushered her past the opening, and indicated the way through a narrow passageway which she guessed correctly opened out into the main hallway at the front of the house.

She had a fleeting impression of light and space, for through the upper glazing of the main door she could see that the front porch doorway was thrown open, and she caught a glimpse of a wide grey-stoned balustrade and steps leading away down. A large bowl of fresh flowers sat on the well-polished surface of a long, mahogany hall table; she could smell their scent filling the air. Her host hurried her past them affording her no time to linger and inhale the delicate fragrance as she would have liked. Her curiosity was awakening to the old house and, when he ushered her into a small drawing room, she could not stop herself exclaiming with delight how lovely it was.

'I'm glad you appreciate something of mine,' he murmured. 'This has always been called the morning-room. Take a seat, I won't be a moment.'

She barely heard him, engrossed with her surroundings. Comfortable wing-backed chairs upholstered in traditional William Morris prints were arranged around the small red-bricked fireplace which, this fine July morning, remained unlit and, instead, a massive arrangement of more fresh flowers and greenery stood on the hearth. Across the thick pile of an oriental rug stood a small matching linen-covered sofa; tables of antique pine stood conveniently nearby. Against one wall, was a large glass-fronted display cabinet, filled with oriental china. In contrast to such a richness of colour, the walls of the room were plain, apart from a collection of watercolours which caught her eye, local scenes she guessed, done with a professional hand she observed critically, taking a closer look. She turned back, to take a seat, choosing one of the wing-backed chairs, and settled herself down, admiring the view from one of the two large recessed windows which looked out on to the well-manicured lawns that sloped endlessly down out of view.

Footsteps crossed the hall, and Lucy looked up expectantly. The woman she had seen earlier entered, carrying a tray with coffee pot and cups, along with a linen-covered basket of rolls accompanied by a dish filled with curls of butter and beside that a pot of conserves.

'Joel won't be long, there was a telephone call for him.' She set the tray down on one of the tables and rearranged the others so that Lucy had one for herself. 'There now, I've popped some fresh rolls on the tray – just in case you fancy a bite.' She smiled at Lucy. 'I'm Winnie Heskett, my husband, Andrew, is Joel's shepherd. We live in one of the cottages on the fell.'

'Oh! Is that near Rose Cottage, Mrs Heskett?' Lucy asked politely, aware the older woman was taking in every inch of her, making her aware that she was hardly dressed for breakfast, however light, taken in this lovely country home, and that she had not even stopped to wash her face or comb her hair after tumbling out of her bed. She bit her lips, thinking Joel Mortimer seemed not to mind. He had wanted her to come in with him, desired her company, it seemed, despite her lack of grooming. Winnie Heskett, on the other hand, looked as if she had risen hours ago, her white hair was neatly pinned back in a bun, not a wisp out of place, but her small blue eyes had a kind look and there was a smile on her bare lips as she shook her head, bending over the tray to serve the coffee.

'Call me, Winnie, I prefer it. Our home? No, dear me no – opposite direction to your little place, but you'll soon find your bearings. I hear you arrived last night.'

'Yes. My name's Lucy – Lucy Elliot.'

Winnie nodded. 'Pleased to meet you Mrs Elliot.'

Lucy frowned. 'It's Miss not Mrs – but' – with a tentative smile on her lips – 'I'd much rather you called me, Lucy.'

Winnie's smile faded slightly, registering visible surprise, and Lucy's smile faltered too, while she wondered if she had misjudged the inviting friendliness of Joel's housekeeper and that she preferred to leave things on a more formal basis, as she heard her say, 'Oh, but I—'

She stopped abruptly as a man's voice startled them both. 'That's fine, Winnie, I think we can manage.' Joel Mortimer stepped aside to let Winnie through the open door, his dismissal tempered with such a warm smile that Lucy noted with surprise how it managed to transform his harsh face so thoroughly. She studied him, pleased with this new, freshly intriguing notion.

They were left alone, and Joel turned his back for a moment while he helped himself to his own coffee. He had discarded the sweater, and the dark polo shirt emphasized that hard, muscular frame she had so perfectly imagined in his shower. His dark hair was slightly dishevelled, Lucy observed, as if he had roughly raked his fingers through it to neaten it. She pressed her hands together, her palms tingling at the sudden desire to run her own through it. The tip of her tongue emerged from her dry mouth, and she unconsciously moistened her lips, irritated that she had not even a scrap of lipstick with which to paint her mouth – recalling one of her casual diktats that a woman could get by without most cosmetics but never her lipstick. How true that stood this morning, she thought idly, when the sun snatched its chance through the broken cloud and filled the room with fresh warmth and light, highlighting the exotic patterns on the rug and energizing the print covering the furnishings but exposing her bare, unmade-up face and especially revealing her naked, unpainted lips.

Lost in thought, she had not noticed that the man had turned back. She caught his gaze upon her and struggled for inner composure, shuffling her feet more tightly together. How could she sit with any elegance in this superb room dressed like this? The chain-store cotton leggings bought in New York had looked the very thing at the time, but they were way past their sell-by date, and her T-shirt was three sizes too big, but that had not seemed to matter when she was supposed to be on vacation, messing about in the countryside, as her brother so charmingly put it when making the invitation. She had not considered that she had to put on a show – for anyone. Now it seemed to matter a great deal!

The thought irritated her composure. She fidgeted and reached over for the cup that Winnie had placed nearby, thinking how well-groomed and perfectly dressed she usually appeared, due to the demands of her particular profession. Her colleagues, not to mention Lucy herself, were veritable fashion plates in the office, surrounded by the paraphernalia, and acquiring the nous that everyone expected, working with and mingling among, the most fashion conscious of the Western world. Her fingers were clumsy around the delicate bone-china handle. The cup rocked in the saucer spilling hot liquid across her hand.

'Oh no!' She sucked in her breath and stared at it like an idiot.

His reflexes were much quicker, setting down his cup on her table with one hand while his other steadied hers, and righted the cup. For a big man his movements were amazingly light and sure. He turned to the tray and reached for the linen cover, dabbing her hand dry. 'I don't think there's any damage,' he said while she stared at him, appalled at what she had done. Her skin felt scorched, not by any means by the hot liquid for that had soon cooled, but by the press of his fingers where he had grasped her hand. Her heart was thumping against her rib-cage so wildly that she was glad of the bagginess of her T-shirt or he would surely see her heightened reaction. Lucy swallowed with difficulty because he made no effort to release her fingers, indeed the light pressure of them was becoming more than bearable, while he bent over to examine her hand. She dragged her eyes from examining the short thick sweep of his lashes and turned to the side table where some of the coffee had fallen.

'Look what I've done!'

He wiped up the mess in an instant with the linen. 'You've done nothing that can't be cleaned up.' He flipped the cloth back on the tray and made for the door. 'I'll ask Winnie for a fresh cup.'

'No! Don't!' Her voice was shrill; it made him stop and turn to look at her more keenly. 'I – er – there's still coffee in the cup. Here' – she raised it to her lips and gulped – 'this is fine – please don't bother.' The coffee obstructed her throat, she had taken such a swig at it, but she concealed the fact, swallowing carefully, wishing she had never accepted the offer to come indoors with him. She had done nothing but make a fool of herself. She bent her head to take another sip, watching him through the veiled sweep of her lashes when he moved back to sit down on the chair opposite.

'Tell me about yourself,' he invited, sipping his coffee. 'I've never met a fashion journalist before. Do you like it?'

'I love it.'

He raised his eyebrows. 'I expect you travel a lot – because of the nature of your work.'

'Yes, I love doing that. Paris – Milan – London.' She grinned. 'It isn't all glamorous though – behind those scenes there can be a battle royal raging – I've observed a few.'

He smiled. 'Do you cover men's fashion too?'

'But, of course. Fashion is fashion regardless of sex.' She stopped; the use of that last word had her mind reeling on a tangent of ideas, and she could picture this tall, very sexy man dressed in the latest world-famous Armani collection she had pre-viewed last spring for the magazine. It made her gabble, expressing her opinions about the latest French ideas, but she soon warmed to her subject, her favourite subject, and he was an artful interrogator, his questions making her dip into the broad experience she had gained over the last few years, until, she realized with breathlessness that she must have talked about herself quite a lot, and exposed to him most of the stages of her working career.

She was telling him how difficult it had been when she had changed her job from newspapers into magazines, explaining the challenges she had met in creating features from her own ideas, when she faltered slightly out of breath. 'Golly!' she admitted while he used the moment to get up and refill their cups, the rolls, untouched by both of them, ignored on the tray. 'You really had me going there – I must have bored the seat of your pants off you!' she exclaimed, forgetting herself, relaxed at last, and at ease.

'Not at all,' he murmured. 'It sounds very

refreshing to listen to you – and I must admit, I had not thought fashionwear a particular subject that would excite my senses, but you have a way with words. Let's say I'm impressed.'

He bent over her with her coffee and set it down on the table beside her. Her cheeks began to tingle with heat so that she lowered her head, on the pretence of re-examining the laces on her Reeboks, knowing that this man certainly did that to her – excited her senses. Since breaking up with Larry a year ago, there had been no one who could do that. She had prided herself on her immunity. Two meetings with this man and he had breached most of her defences, so much so that, here she was imagining him naked, imagining a lot worse than that, resurrecting feelings she had long denied herself. Her heartbeats quickened and she felt the familiar dryness invade her mouth.

She stood up, knowing she needed to get out of here soon. 'Look, I think I'd better be getting back – they must be stirring by now – and they'll both be wondering where on earth I am.'

'I suppose you're right,' he agreed, glancing at his wristwatch and frowning. 'I was enjoying myself so much I lost track of the time. I have to go too. How long do you plan to stay at the cottage?'

'I'm not sure – I told Peter a week, maybe two. How long has he rented it for?'

'Two months.' Joel looked up sharply. 'Didn't he tell you that?'

Lucy shrugged. 'I never thought to ask. I can only stay two weeks at the most. After that I'll have to get back to London – and into work.'

'Then I wish you a pleasant stay here.' He looked at her rather strangely, and she felt the ground gained in the last few minutes in his morning-room had suddenly been wiped out.

For something to say, to stop it happening she asked, 'This estate – it keeps you busy?' while moving to the door, as he followed closely behind her.

'It keeps my manager very busy. As a matter of fact I have other business to attend to down in London later this afternoon.'

'Oh!' It disappointed her that he delegated his business to others. For a landowner he did not look the sort of man who spent most of his life in idle pleasure. She judged him to be in his early thirties, and his intelligence and business sense had left her quite impressed, for he had thrust several keen questions concerning the particular world in which her life revolved, and it had quite surprised her.

She glanced around the room before leaving, and for the first time wondered if he was married. The place had a feminine touch, someone with taste, she acknowledged, someone who cared about the place. Yet she had not the nerve to ask if he had a wife. She did not dare. Knowing him, he would guess the reason behind it. She passed by the bowl of roses on the hall table, and thought of the fresh arrangement in the room they had both just left. Women's touches – Winnie's touches, perhaps? Maybe – or was there a Mrs Mortimer taking her breakfast in bed, she wondered? Gazing up the stairs as he waited for her to follow him back through the passage. He caught her glance and for a long moment their eyes locked. His eyebrows jiggled, for once misinterpreting her thoughts, so that she blushed heavily, annoyed with him as much as herself. How many times had she made a fool of herself in the space of an hour! She could not wait to get back to her car and away from him.

Peter and Sophia, both dressed in jeans and shirts, were ploughing through bowls of cereal at the small square-shaped dining-table that stood under the open staircase when she walked in. Lucy had had plenty of time to compose herself on the short drive back down the track.

'Where've you been?' her brother asked, his mouth full of cornflakes.

'Up at the Hall with Joel Mortimer. He asked me in for coffee.'

'Oh yes?' He stopped chewing.

'What's that supposed to mean?'

'You tell me.'

'Stop making an issue, Peter; I had to drive the man back after all.'

'He has an army of staff to do that for him.'

Lucy thought it timely to deflect his line of conversation. 'You're rather surly this fine summer morning, didn't you sleep well?' And without waiting for a reply she turned to the child. 'Did you sleep well, Sophia?' To which the child nodded a little shyly. 'Well, I could do with some of that.' She escaped into the kitchen to make her own breakfast.

Peter was like a dog with a bone as he called out, 'Didn't he offer you something up there – with the coffee?'

'I could have had something, but I wasn't hungry – then.'

'Oh! He makes you lose your appetite – that's interesting.'

Lucy groaned as she poured cereal in her bowl and retrieved some milk from the fridge. 'Shut up, Peter. The subject is closed.'

'That suits me – where he's concerned.'

'Peter!' She eyeballed him coming back into the room to join them at the table.

'OK. What do you want to do today?' he asked instead.

'Well,' – she tasted the cornflakes and crunched into them for a few moments, – 'judging by the bare cupboards in there, I suggest we find the local Sainsbury's and do a mega shop.'

'We've been eating out mostly.'

'I can see that. There's some bread in the stone crock that's decidedly green in colour. What a parent!'

'I don't like bread!' Sophia commented.

Lucy's eyes flashed at her brother. 'I can understand that – judging the stale offerings your papa has in store.'

'Papa takes me to the Happy Eater – I like hamburgers!'

'Happy Eater?'

'It's a diner not too far away.'

'Well we can sort out some shopping and maybe have some lunch in the village later,' Lucy suggested.

Peter pulled out his wallet from his jeans pocket and withdrew a few notes from it. 'Can I leave the shopping to you? I haven't a clue – take Sophia with you – she can choose what she likes.'

Lucy glanced over at his daughter. 'I'm not sure about giving Sophia a free rein in selecting the food – but I'm happy to have you come with me. That is if you want to?'

The small voice quavered with uncertainty. 'I don't know. Where are you going, Papa?'

Lucy's heart contracted at the obvious feeling of

insecurity in the child's world. She flashed him an
angry look which he totally ignored. Peter's little
trips out to the local hostelry had not exactly
helped.

'I'm heading down the village for a decent
morning paper.'

'Can I come with you instead?' Sophia asked
eagerly.

He stood up, carrying his dirty bowl to the
kitchen, looking over his shoulder at Sophia. 'Have
you washed and brushed your teeth yet?'

She was up in a flash, half the cereal left uneaten.
'It won't take me a moment.' Without waiting for
his response she scrambled up the stairs for the
bathroom as fast as her little legs could take her.

'I'll see you later then,' her brother said. 'Can I
ask you to see to the shopping? You'll be much
better than me in choosing the stuff. Women
always are.'

'Sexist!' Lucy remarked without heat.

He grinned. 'It's got me by – over the years.'

'I can imagine – those pity-me eyes of yours have
a lot to answer for. Just remember what we were
talking about last night. Your girlfriends can't help
you out of this responsibility – and I am only here
another two weeks at the most. I've already used up
part of my vacation when I stayed with my friend,
Monique, in Brittany.'

Sophia was back in no time. 'I'm ready, Papa.'
Peter picked up his car keys from the mantelshelf.
The child flashed her aunt a broad cheeky grin,
''Bye Lucy.'

After she heard the roar of Peter's ancient MG
disappear up the track she leaned back in her chair
and her eyes swept the room in disgust. It really

LAKE PARK PUBLIC LIBRARY

33155

was a pretty little cottage, low-beamed with white
plastered walls, thick, deepset windows with
cheerful cotton curtains and views that swept the
fells. But the room was a study in chaos. Peter had
no idea how to keep a place tidy. There were
discarded clothes, old newspapers and – worst of
all – the remains of a take-away meal in an
aluminium container, that must have been a couple
of days old, standing on the hearth. She wrinkled
her nose with distaste, and worried that his habits
might have already attracted a few uninvited mice.
She supposed she would have to make a start on
cleaning the place, and considered tackling it now,
while they were down in the village. She looked
around her, wondering where to begin, and
glanced at one of the pictures on the wall. It
depicted the view from the window. She stood up
to have a closer look and discovered it had a similar
style as the collection in Joel's morning-room. The
signature was obscure, and she could not make it
out, but it made her think about Joel Mortimer
with disturbing clarity.

It was harder than she thought, an hour later,
and she mused that Peter was taking quite some
time on an errand that should have lasted only a
few minutes. No doubt he had rootled out a beauty
spot in which to sit and study his newspaper in
peace, while his sister sorted out the cottage. First
there had been the fire; cleaning it out had been a
dirty business, and she had discovered more
distasteful take-away evidence stuffed in the coal
skuttle. Neither could she find any rubber gloves to
protect her hands. Consequently it had taken her
quite some time to scrub them clean after she had
emptied the grate of ash and cinders. The old

vacuum cleaner she discovered in the cupboard had freshened up the carpet, and polishing up the dining-table had worked wonders. She had even dashed out into the small apology of a garden to snip off some sprigs of honeysuckle and fill a jug with them which she had found in the kitchen. Placing them finally on the table she smiled with the pleasure their sight and scent brought her.

She was beginning to sort out the kitchen when there was a light rap on the door. Assuming Peter and Sophia had returned she hurried out to greet them, waiting for their exclamations of appreciation at the miracles she had wrought on the old place.

The door was open, just as she had left it when she had returned with the honeysuckle. A man stood on the threshold. He was very tall, so lean he looked emaciated. His hair was grey and straggly, and he had a wild look in his eyes. His old corduroy trousers looked a little the worse for wear and his checked flannel shirt was frayed around the cuffs. He was holding a plastic carrier bag in his hand and Lucy thought immediately of vagrants. She had seen enough of them in London; her heart thumped with unease. She glanced back at the kitchen, knowing she could not get rid of him with a donation of food for there was none to give until she went out for that dratted shopping – and she knew the folly of looking for her purse, relieved she had stuffed Peter's money out of sight.

'You the lady of the house?' he rasped abruptly.

Four

'Yes.' She glanced back at the kitchen. 'Do you want to see my husband?' pretending that that particular fictional image was nearby.

'I called in at the Hall. My wife asked me to drop by and bring this down. She thought you might appreciate it. I'm Andrew Heskett.'

'The shepherd!' She ignored his abruptness and sagged with relief against the wall, clutching the duster and polish in front of her.

'I can see you're busy and I must get on – I'll leave this then.' He moved indoors and dropped the bag on to the table.

She stared at it for some moments before moving to peer into it. There was a basket of eggs, and a paper bag filled with fresh rolls of bread.

'Why! How kind of your wife to—' She looked up and realized the man had already left. She ran out of the door and looked down the fell, but he was nowhere to be seen. She ran round the side of the cottage and gazed up the steep roughened track, and was just in time to note his tall, thin figure disappear into the thick woods that bordered the edge of a grazing paddock at the rear of the cottage, a black and white collie dog at his heel.

Her eyes quickened with interest. There was so

much to see here, the track through the woods, for instance, and the wildness of the fell to trace. No doubt, Joel's shepherd knew every square inch of it. She wondered if Joel's knowledge of his own land was as familiar as Andrew Heskett's. She ached to explore.

It was nearly noon when Peter's car could be heard roaring down the track. He emerged from the garage with Sophia without apology. The coffee shop down in the village had proved an irresistible attraction. Especially when one of the customers from the local inn had been about to enter as he walked past, his errands done, and she, on a similar pursuit, had invited them to join her. Sophia had not minded. There had been another child – Peter's friend was a divorcee with a lively nine-year-old girl. Sophia had found company and diversion from well-meaning adults.

'Actually she's invited us all to lunch tomorrow. It's a short drive along the valley,' he explained. 'Quite a remote place, by all accounts. But Susan's a lovely woman; you'll like her.'

'I want to go and play with Caroline,' Sophia said firmly.

'Caroline?' Lucy queried.

'She's my new friend.'

'Susan's daughter,' Peter explained quickly.

'She's got a pony called Sparky. She said she'd teach me to ride him.'

'I'm not sure about that one, poppet,' her father said. 'I'm not keen on horses.'

'I'm not surprised,' Lucy retorted. Explaining to the child. 'He got a nasty fright when he was just a little older than you – his friend's pony bolted with him on it. He was thrown and suffered a broken collar bone.'

'I certainly do not fear them,' Peter said with spirit. 'I rode Blackie again as soon as my bones mended, I merely treat them now with a healthy respect.'

'Exactly – a healthy distance, in your case.'

Sophia was not put off. 'I like ponies. I'd love to ride one.'

'We'll see,' her father promised.

In the event, Lucy shopped alone, after they had all lunched together down at the local pub, much to Sophia's disappointment who was expecting her usual supply of burger and chips at the Happy Eater, a diner some distance away. Nevertheless, the meals were good, and even Sophia appreciated the special children's menu and was persuaded to try their cowboy pie, which thankfully proved a great success. Afterwards, Lucy decided to obtain provisions in the village, as she eyed the few shops across the green. Peter intended to take a drive up the Kirkstone Pass to admire the view of Ullswater and maybe take some snapshots. Sophia thought this a more exciting adventure than being dragged along by her aunt for an hour or two and elected to join him instead. Lucy would have preferred to take the scenic route too, but there were immediate supplies to be had with which they could not do without up at the cottage. She waved them off from the pub's private car-park and set off to walk across the green.

There was less cloud now and it was becoming warmer. She shrugged out of her blazer and let the sun's rays play on her bare arms and legs. Her short, navy-coloured pleated skirt swung against her thighs as she strode out across the grass, and the soft, silk, cream top she had chosen as a more appropriate outfit in which to dine out was quite effective against her honey-coloured skin, agonizingly acquired, because her fair skin was difficult to tan, during her two weeks of sunshine on the Brittany coast. Thankfully she had discarded heels for a more sensible pair of flat shoes and, as she hurried across, she rummaged in her shoulder bag for her sunglasses, slipping them on as she neared the edge of the path which trailed the green, thinking guiltily that the springing, weedless turf was never meant for walking across, noticing for the first time the formal rose borders and belatedly the small sign specifically asking visitors not to walk on the grass.

She quickened her step and crossed the road where cars were parked almost bumper to bumper, glad that she had left her own car back at the pub. She could always drive over to pick up her groceries later, she decided, slipping into the nearest shop which held an attractive display of local crafts in its large window. It was also a coffee shop. There were not many tables, crammed as they were at the rear of the ground floor near a large bay window which overlooked an attractive garden area, but they were fully taken by customers. A young girl was threading her way through the tables to take a fresh order. Lucy glanced across in a friendly manner as she fingered a rack of brightly coloured silk scarves. Her eyes stilled, and she slipped off her sunglasses as she recognized one of the women. Winnie Heskett's eyes missed nothing, and she lifted her hand and beckoned her over.

'Come and join us for a cup of tea or something,

won't you?' she invited as Lucy stepped across to say a polite hello. The woman was with two others, curiosity gleaming in their friendly eyes. 'Sit down.'

'Oh, we've just had lunch – I haven't room for anything else. I have some errands to do – but thanks all the same.'

'Have they left you on your own?'

Three pairs of eyes scanned the empty space behind her. Lucy nodded. 'Peter's taken Sophia up the Kirkstone Pass for a ride out.'

'It's fine enough for the view, the day,' commented one of the ladies, seemingly interested in the brevity of Lucy's skirt as she ran her gaze down her legs.

Winnie felt introductions were necessary. 'This is Lucy Elliot.' She shot Lucy an old-fashioned look as she stressed the next word. '*Miss* Elliot – and this is Emily Standon and her sister Ethel, friends of mine who live here in the village.'

Lucy smiled. 'Hello, I must say I think your village is lovely, the little I've seen of it so far.'

'Going over Kirkstone Pass for the first time is quite impressive. didn't you want to go with them?' asked Winnie, after glancing darkly at Ethel, aggrieved that her friend was pointedly staring at the younger woman's hemline.

'I would have loved to, but I need to get some things – oh, that reminds me, thanks for the parcel you sent up. It was very kind of you.'

'Andrew told me he'd called.' Winnie looked thoughtful for a moment. 'Any time you need some eggs just call down at the Hall.'

'I will.' Feeling she was intruding on what looked like a good afternoon of gossip, she used the excuse of her shopping to take her leave. She sauntered down the street outside, pausing to glance in the shop windows, enjoying herself like any other tourist.

The village store was small, but packed with everything she wanted. She had to jostle with others, and wait a lengthy time at the inadequate check-out till. The bags were getting heavier by the time she was halfway round the path that circled the green. She dropped her sunglasses just as she was about to cross the road, nearly causing a traffic accident as she stooped to pick them up hearing the screech of brakes behind her while staring helplessly as three cartons of milk and two sticks of bread slithered out of one of the carriers and spilled into a nearby gutter. Lucy cursed softly, aware of the blast of a car horn which increased her annoyance. She blithely ignored it and attempted to restack the goods back into the bag only to find the oranges and apples were rolling happily out of the other.

'Give me a break!' she muttered crossly, crouching afresh to retrieve the fruit.

A shadow crossed her path. 'Having trouble?'

His voice was enough to shatter her co-ordination. Her limbs felt like water, she groped for an apple, her fingers clawing air instead. Joel Mortimer picked up the offending fruit and offered it to her.

'Not forbidden, I trust!' His joke seemed to fall upon deaf ears. She frowned, looking up, the sunlight blinding her eyes. He was a dark predator hovering over her, and she, the prey, caught in his snare. Her heart was pounding like a brick against her sides, and she felt her throat dry with excitement.

No one reduced her to this, or no one had until now, she thought wildly, and bent her head, intent on her task. She slipped on her sunglasses, her eyes safely shielded from his blue, intent gaze. The heat in her cheeks could be explained by the force of her actions, and only she was to know of the inner consternation that fired her blood, then prickled her skin with an intense but spontaneous reaction towards him. He should be in London. It was early afternoon. He had informed her himself that he intended travelling down there – today. One thought careered into another as she blindly attended to her bags. Unless he had easy access to air transport he could never have made the journey and return so soon.

'It's rather uncanny how we keep meeting in the middle of roads,' he mentioned, bending over, swiftly relieving her of her bags. 'Do you know I could have caused you a serious injury – or worse! Didn't you hear my horn?'

'Oh it was you? Yes! I heard.' She snatched one of the bags from him. 'Do you mind? I can manage without your help.'

'That wasn't the case last night,' he reminded her affably.

'No,' she agreed, 'but that was then and this is now!'

'Mr Mortimer – Lucy!' Winnie Heskett almost trotted across the green, her ample bosom heaving with exercise. 'Is everything all right? I heard the brakes, and I thought – oh, dear me!' Her round face pink with exertion. 'I hurried across as fast as I could.'

'Don't have palpitations, Winnie. Lucy fancied a game of bowling with her greengroceries in the middle of the road, that's all.'

Winnie stared with total incomprehension. Lucy giggled. Joel grinned at them both. Lucy thought he looked like a young boy, the expression so totally transformed his usual forbidding features. Forbidding! Was that how she saw him? No, she amended, dangerous – that was more like it. Her senses recorded it.

There was danger in his voice, for it was so startlingly attractive. There was danger in his eyes, for he could look at her so intently, as if he could read her soul. Danger in his thoughts, for they were, so far, incomprehensible to her. Yet his thoughts mattered, all of them, especially about herself. And she knew that he harboured some, her instinct alone told her that. It excited her. She remembered the way their bodies had pressed together in that one breathless second when she had clung to him in his rain-swept yard. She had known excitement. Danger and excitement, the words intertwined, and associated themselves with Joel Mortimer. Danger, because she could not stop her own reactions, and therefore her control, and excitement, because that was exactly how she felt – excited.

'The others have left her to drive up Kirkstone. Poor lass has to get the groceries in – typical that is. Men! They're all alike,' Winnie snorted, and wrinkled her nose.

'Do you need a lift back, Winnie?' he asked her.

'No. Andrew said he'd call by at the Stantons'. We're having supper there. Don't worry about me.' She glanced at Lucy. 'As long as the lass looks OK – I'll be off.' And she was, moving along the path without a backwards glance. Lucy stared at Joel, her bags clutched in front of her like a shield.

'Can I offer you a lift?' he asked.

'I thought you were due in London?' she countered instead.

'It was cancelled.'

'It?' she pressed.

'The meeting.'

'What meeting?'

'My meeting,' he finished testily. 'You are a remarkably nosy female.'

'It's my job.'

'Of course. How forgetful of me. Can I give you a lift?'

'No thanks. My car's parked down at the pub.'

'I see. Then perhaps I can carry those down there for you.' He was already moving, his hands urging the bags away from her fingers. Lucy gave them over; that danger and excitement pumping the adrenalin madly through her body.

They walked the short distance to the car-park. Joel handed the bags over as soon as she opened the side door of her Renault. Lucy deposited them on the back seat. Even then, the offending fruit tumbled out and rolled about on the car floor. Joel looked at her and smiled. Her heart melted, and her insides boiled with heat. *Danger. Excitement.* Lucy caught her lower lip between her teeth and discovered her hands were trembling so much she dropped her linen jacket as she hitched her shoulder bag more firmly upon her shoulders. He stooped to pick it up at the same time as she. Their fingers touched. They almost stroked. Lucy could have screamed. This was not happening, she said to herself. This was a dream!

'I suppose I'll see you again.'

'Wha-at!' she stammered out.

'Out and about,' he replied. 'You said you were staying for a couple of weeks. We're bound to bump into one another – allowing for the fact that you are staying in one of my cottages.'

'Oh! Of course.'

He seemed reluctant to go. 'Don't you mind being left on your own?'

'What do you mean?'

'The others – your, er.' He paused, and she had the incredible notion that this man could not bring himself to say Peter's name for some reason. Her brother must have made a distinctly unhealthy impression in the few days he had lived in Rose Cottage.

'Yes?' she prompted. 'What about them?'

'The man and his child – leaving you like this.'

She laughed. 'Of course not. I prefer being on my own. I like it. Anyway, I'll be back with them later, won't I?'

'I suppose that's your choice.' And with that he turned and left her. She watched his tall figure cross the green and take possession of his car. Not the Range Rover of last night but a Mercedes sports model. She watched him ease it out into the steady stream of traffic. He glanced her way as he drove past, his eyes hidden behind dark glasses, but his hand lifted in a friendly salute which she totally ignored, pretending to search inside her bag for her keys instead, but her eyes were upon him, surreptitiously between lowered lids, watching the dark green car disappear from her vision.

It was not until she reached the cottage that she realized she had no keys to get in. Peter had not returned, the garage was empty. She glanced at her watch. It was later than she thought. They would surely not be long. She waited ten minutes and then started up her engine, crashing the gears with some force as she headed back up the track to the Hall. In the cobbled yard she braked to a halt. She glanced across the outbuildings. His manager would surely have a spare set of keys. She should have thought to ask for them earlier when Joel had persuaded her in for coffee. She got out of the car and wandered across to the office. The door was closed, she peered inside the window. It was empty. The place looked totally deserted.

'Can I help you?'

Her spine stiffened, her senses signalled action – on red alert. She spun round and stared at him from across the yard. That kitchen doorway was becoming increasingly familiar. 'I'm locked out,' she explained without preamble, 'I wonder if I might have another set of keys.'

'No problem.' He sauntered over. She could not avoid the eye contact. There was nowhere else to look which would not seem artificially contrived. Suddenly her skirt seemed three inches too short. She felt his eyes on her lower limbs. Heat seeped through the skin.

'I realize I should have obtained my own keys earlier—'

His dark eyes were very slow as they moved upwards until they reached her face. He examined her mouth for some seconds before commenting, 'If you like being on your own, then I imagine that's a good idea.'

She wondered if he was being cynical. He did not smile, and yet, those last few moments had her lips tingling, and he deliberately did not raise his gaze. Her mouth felt stung and swollen. She was the first to turn away. What was he doing? What was she doing allowing him to look at her like that?

'Why don't you wait in the house.'

'No!' she said sharply.

'It could be some time.'

'I know.' She stood her ground. 'Look, can you help me or not? Have you a spare set of keys?'

'They'll be in the office – and it's locked. Manny could be anywhere.'

She turned back angrily and stared at him, forcing down the panic that swelled in her throat, managing this time not to allow that disturbing scrutiny to get under her skin. 'I'm sure you're the type of man who knows exactly where your members of staff should or should not be.'

'You make me sound rather autocratic – I can assure you I'm not.'

'Really Mr—' His eyebrows shot up warningly. 'Joel,' she amended hastily, 'don't you think we've rather deviated from the subject?'

'You have plenty of time – I can't get into Manny's cottage to get your keys just yet because he's checking out some fences down by the roadway. But I know he'll be back in a few minutes.' He held out an arm. 'Let me show you round the yard while we wait.'

'Oh I—'

'I'm sure you'd love to show little Sophia around the stables sometime when you're passing through. It'll be a pleasant diversion for the child and you have my permission.'

She felt stupid and stammered with confusion, 'Wh-why thank you – she would love that.'

'Does she ride?'

He ushered her past the row of ancient

redbricked outbuildings and indicated she step
through an narrow arched opening she had not
noticed, tucked away in a small embrasure round
the corner. 'No,' Lucy answered, recalling Sophia's
admission that her new friend might teach her
tomorrow.

'Do you?'

'Not since I was a child, I'm afraid.'

'Perhaps you might like to ride out sometime
while you're here.'

'Oh, I think not; I expect I'd be a bit rusty in the
saddle these days.' The very idea made her
chuckle.

'Nonsense – we might have a hack out together,
how would you like that?' She did not dare to reply.
Danger and excitement were wreaking havoc
inside her.

They were beautiful horses, she ackowledged, as
he led her past the rear of the courtyard towards a
large enclosed paddock. There were eight of them
grazing in a group, their bodies sleek and shining
with health. Easily the biggest, an iron-grey mare,
raised her head as soon as they emerged from the
other side of the embrasure and whinnied in
recognition of her master, trotting over with all the
confidence of a well-loved mount. She nuzzled
Joel's palm as he offered her a Polo Mint.

'She's lovely,' Lucy said softly, unable to resist
running her hand down her proud bent neck.

'She is,' admitted Joel, just as softly, and she
looked up and found his eyes not on the mare but
on her. His mouth spread in a slow, provokingly
sensual smile.

Beating hooves vibrated the ground in the
distance. They sounded as loud as the heartbeats

echoing in her ears as they drew nearer. The others, not to be ignored, cantered across, providing a welcome distraction as she stroked their enquiring noses, while they shuffled for positions around the man and woman.

Lucy's brain was spinning with crazy conjecture. He was flirting with her, and she was beginning to like it.

Five

The horses hustled for attention and, over the shifting quarters and beyond thrown heads, she could see a car moving at fast speed down below on the valley road. It was Peter's small racer. She glanced back at Joel, appreciating his strong distinctive profile outlined against the sky; his thick hair was lifting from his brow, tousled and boyish, but his jaw was tight, and the smile suddenly disappeared. He had seen the car too, and her spirits dropped at his reaction. What was it between him and her brother? She wanted them to at least be tolerant of one another. Instead she sensed this *friction.*

'I must go,' she said a little regretfully.

'I suppose so,' he agreed, and she nearly imagined he felt the same.

'It was kind of you to show me your horses.'

'Kind?' His mouth thinned as he added, 'Hardly!'

'I don't understand—' Then suddenly she stopped, she did understand and that fiery temper of hers unleashed itself. 'You don't have to entertain me in your own valuable time. I'm not a child – I can contain my patience, you know – I would have sat in my car waiting for your manager

68

to eventually turn u—'

His voice was harsh cutting her off abruptly, 'I wasn't patronizing – believe me.'

The horses whickered impatiently, stretching their necks over the fencing for attention, their nostrils vibrating, velvet mouths seeking Polos as one nibbled innocently against Lucy's bare arm. Joel stepped forward, ignoring the iron-grey who favoured him, and reached over to tap one of the bays, who was reaching for another piece of Lucy's arm, on the nose.

'Don't, Sabre,' he commanded, the anger still in him, 'that's enough.'

It seemed his emotion was catching, or was it from her, for the grey mare's ears flattened and she curled her powerful neck round to grab a piece of the bay's flesh with her teeth. Lucy jumped with fright. Joel's arms caught her firmly and pulled her away from the fence out of reach of suddenly bared teeth, rolling eyes and stamping hooves.

'Jealous beggars,' he muttered, his breath stroking her cheek. This time, more loudly in his admonishment to his mare, 'Stop that, Sheba.' The grey whickered, acknowledging her name, knowing she belonged to him and ignoring the herd shook her wonderful mane and snorted, lifting her head to reach over for his attention. 'You'll have your moment, madam,' her master promised, 'another time – but not today.'

Lucy felt the shiver feather her spine. He released her at once, and she tingled where the warmth of his hands had touched. No wonder the mare danced before him, she decided, shuffling her own feet uncomfortably, trying to place herself some distance from him. His attraction was deadly.

She had no control over it and neither, Lucy concluded, did his horses, prancing like children for attention, clustering together, hind quarters clashing gently, tails swishing with impatience. She forgot her sudden rise of temper. 'You know exactly how to treat them,' she smiled. 'It's amazing!'

'I appreciate their qualities and love them – and in return, they love me,' he stated with simplicity and without a hint of arrogance.

'Yes. I can believe that.'

His eyes searched her face, but the smile had vanished from his. 'The offer of a ride out still stands – my animals would love some extra exercise, you know.'

'Thanks, but I don't know about that. I'm too inexperienced.' She eyed the fickle scrum on the other side of the fence.

'I'll have Manny send down your keys,' he said, continuing to stroke the horses' heads and offer their eager, greedy mouths more mints without turning round.

In an instant Lucy felt dismissed. 'As you like.' She fled, heading through the embrasure without daring to glance back.

Peter and Sophia had already reached the cottage when she turned her car down the track. They helped her indoors with the groceries, poking their noses inside to see what kind of food she had bought for them. Sophia was bursting to tell her how high she had climbed when they had stopped at the top of the pass.

'It was like being on top of the world, Lucy, I told Papa that we should have made you come with us instead.'

'Was it really? Then I shall have to go another time,' Lucy told her, bending down to supply the fridge with fresh butter and eggs, while all the time her attention was centred on Joel's strange withdrawal and she wondered ceaselessly what she had done to be the cause of it.

After a light supper, which Lucy prepared herself, Peter stayed with them instead of sloping off to the pub. They even played a game of Monopoly at which Sophia cheated outrageously. There was a great deal of laughter and her father cannily upstaged her by swindling her out of her 'money' at the end of the game. There was such an uproar from Sophia when she discovered the counter plot that Lucy nearly missed hearing the light knock on the cottage door. Peter, quietly chuckling to himself, disappeared into the kitchen to make them some cocoa.

It was Joel. His broad shoulders filled the tiny porchway while beyond lay the tranquillity of twilight; birdsong broke spasmodically from nearby, and the scents of the cottage garden drifted in the air. 'I wasn't sure you'd be in.' He glanced at the closed doors of the garage barn. 'Is everything all right?' he asked suddenly.

Lucy frowned with puzzlement. 'Of course it is. Why? Is something wrong?'

He paused a moment. 'It's just that before I knocked there sounded one hell of a racket going on inside – it startled the birds sitting on the climbing rose on top of this porch.'

She laughed softly. 'That was just about the size of things. We're just finishing a game of Monopoly. It was very intense.'

'Oh! I suppose he's left the pair of you for the

pub.' She caught the hard edge in his voice which curbed her smile as he added, 'At least the poor child's not alone this time.'

'Who is it, love?' Peter appeared from behind and draped a casual arm cross his sister's shoulders and looked outside. 'Oh, it's you!' Lucy felt a sudden chill in the air and an oncoming disruption to the peaceful surroundings. 'Is there a problem?'

Sophia pressed her little face to Lucy's free side. 'Hello, Mr Mortimer.' Innocently asking, 'Aren't you coming inside?'

'Yes, of course you are,' said Lucy, the three of them filling the doorway, but the slight hint of pressure from her shoulder against Peter's chest had no effect. He stood obdurately firm, right behind her. It was like pushing against a brick wall. She hoped Joel could not see it. She felt suddenly ashamed of her brother's lack of manners, but Joel's attitude confused her, and the strained atmosphere between the two men did not help. Needles of heat prickled her flesh but she pressed home the invite nonetheless. 'Do come inside.'

'No, thanks all the same. I walked down to bring you these.' He held out a set of keys.

Her brother curled his fingers through his blond hair where it flopped across his forehead. From inside the kettle whistled to the boil. 'Excuse me.' He turned back inside and left Lucy to deal with him. She felt his fingers cool against her half-outstretched hand. Joel dropped the keys into her palm and turned away as if to leave.

She was determined to stop this silly nonsense between the men, and keeping her words light said swiftly and with more warmth, 'It's quite a way down from the Hall. Why don't you share some cocoa with us before going back?' Now that he was here, she wanted him to stay, despite the atmosphere.

'That's very kind of you, but it's getting rather late – and I have some work to finish.' He could have sent Manny as he had said he would; if he was so pressed for time, he could have driven, rather than walk; now, it seemed, he was far too busy to bother himself. He was too polite, and her face stiffened at his indifference. He saw it, but the expression in his eyes was guarded and difficult to assess, even with the light from inside spilling all over his strong, masculine features. 'Maybe another time.'

'Sophia!' Peter called from indoors. 'Bedtime!'

Lucy caught her lower lip between her teeth, and her cheeks coloured at the obvious intention to dissuade their visitor from lingering obvious in her brother's tone of voice. Sophia obediently turned to obey, but hesitated long enough to whisper in a small, breathless voice, 'Goodnight, Mr Mortimer,' and haltingly issued her own invite, 'please come back again – I like you.' She said it so shyly, that, not daring to hear his reply, she dashed back into the house.

'Well, how can I refuse a charming little lady like that?' Joel asked, his teeth gleaming with a sudden revealing smile.

Lucy could not stop herself admitting, 'She's adorable, isn't she?' His smile disappeared and he stared at her long and hard. 'What's the matter?' she asked him, her thoughts whirling. Why was he looking at her like that?

'She favours her father in looks, doesn't she?'

'Very much so,' she agreed.

'She told me she was extremely nervous about meeting you.'

'Did she? Well, I'm not hard to get to know.'

'Aren't you?' His eyes studied her face for a long, breathless moment. 'I must go. Goodnight, Lucy.' She took her time closing the door, watching his tall figure retreat up the track aware that the sound of his voice and the heat in his eyes had stirred her senses in a powerful way.

He was in her dreams, involved in dark disturbing scenes that tantalized her mind so much that the images stayed with her as she awoke the next morning – images of them together. On the way to meet Peter's new friend for lunch, she found herself unable to escape from her thoughts, the detritus of those dreams clung in brief, excited sequences that in spite of how hard she tried, her deep subconscious would not allow her to piece together and make the picture whole. But she knew enough to know they were erotic, bewitching almost, and her senses were engaged in a very real way when she kept drifting into them, unable to control her riotous imagination or the feelings she was experiencing about the man who owned Monk Hall. She was travelling in the old racer beside Peter, while Sophia snuggled down in the back between them; the hood was down, and the wind tugging her hair into a wild tangle thankfully kept the heat from staining her cheeks which had nothing to do with the bright sunshine.

Susan Pallister and her daughter, Caroline, were already waiting for them on the porch of a large old, rambling farmhouse a short distance outside the village of Glenridding round the curve of Lake Ullswater. Her brother pressed the car horn and lifted one hand in a wave, the gestures full of a man who wanted to impress. It was clear to Lucy that Peter's affections went deeper than she first thought.

Susan was a very attractive woman, slightly reserved, quietly spoken; a woman reaching her early thirties, Lucy guessed, with short spiky dark-brown hair and enormous, hazel-coloured eyes which, as the morning progressed, sought her brother's face with monotonous regularity. The children happily entertained themselves, for Caroline, a smaller version of the mother, but with a more bubbling, effervescent personality, tore off past the house to a rolling stretch of meadow with Sophia to meet Sparky.

They had drinks out on a pretty terrace which overlooked the lake. Susan taught in the local primary school where her daughter was also a pupil. They learned that her husband was killed in a farm accident when the child was only a baby. Now their farmland was leased by a neighbouring family, and Susan had held on only to the farmhouse and meadow, an arrangement which suited her financial needs, and enabled her to keep the family home which, she explained, had been lived in by the Pallister family for the last five generations.

'So you feel you have family roots here,' Peter asked, sipping his beer and gazing down seriously at his hostess.

'It's rather nice to have ties, don't you think?'

'Hmm!' Peter buried his nose in the rim of his drink and went quiet.

Lucy grinned at that and her like for the woman increased. 'You have a wonderful old home, Susan,' she ventured, more to change the subject as her brother stared down into the meadow, brooding on his new-found friend's ideas of family ties. They had never been Peter's strong points.

'I count my blessings,' Susan replied rather shortly, suddenly jumping up from the rattan chair to peer down the meadow. 'Where are those girls?'

Lucy wondered if Susan did not wish reminders of her past either, glancing curiously at the lithe figure of the woman as she slipped down the wooden steps which brought her to a pathway made out of slabs of stone that led all the way to the lake. Peter drained his beer and set the glass down on the edge of the terrace rail.

'Why don't you go down and walk with her?' Lucy suggested, watching Susan hurry some distance away, her eyes shaded from the sun, while she scanned the meadow on the lookout for the girls. 'I'll stay here.'

'If you're sure.'

Some time passed before she saw any of them again, and Lucy had discovered the merits of the canopied swing seat. She heard them first. Excited urges from children's voices and the distinct sound of Peter's deep, slow laughter followed by Susan's careful instructions. She guessed Sparky was being put through his paces and, presently, a small very plump pony with a gleaming chestnut coat came into view.

'Oh dear!' Lucy murmured, her hands on the bars, limiting the swing motion to give her whole attention to the parade.

Sophia sat with pride on his sturdy back, her little bare legs clinging like vines around his rotund frame, while Caroline led him, or rather, hauled him across the meadow pulling a lead rein attached to the halter. Sparky glanced out of the corner of his eye at Lucy swinging slowly to a halt on the terrace. She grinned at the harassed animal,

feeling very sorry for the little mount. He looked
very fed up, his nose thrust out with reluctance or
belligerence, with animals it was difficult to assess,
for he was pulled along with a determined air and
his fat belly sagged with motion as he thrust first
one foreleg and then a hindleg and so it went on.
Sophia giggled with pleasure on his back, but she
was oblivious to her mount's reluctance, only
seeing she was riding him, no matter with how
much difficulty. It was pretty obvious that he had
seen little work so far this summer and now that a
rider's demands were being made upon him he
hardly liked it at all.

'Look at me, Lucy, look −!' At that moment
Sparky rebelled, digging his little hooves into the
soft turf and pulling back with all his might. His
rump raised alarmingly and Sophia's face
crumpled with fright, her hands clutching his
rough grey-coloured mane. Peter went chalk-white
as he too staggered to an abrupt halt along with
Susan at Sparky's neck.

'Now then!' Susan spoke with authority and
Sparky's rump flattened at once. 'Walk on,' she
commanded, adding softly, 'Not much further now
boy.'

Caroline, somewhat subdued at her favourite
pony's insubordination, went terribly quiet. The
lead rein slackened, but Sparky was listening to a
higher authority and for Susan he was the model of
manners. His nose perked up, his neck arched and
he swished his tail as instead of walking, he trotted
proudly past, highstepping for some distance
across the front of the terrace, almost as if on
parade. Sophia nearly fell off at that, but quickly
regained her senses to cling steadfastly against his

little squat belly and bobbed past Lucy with a determined grin pasted all over her shining face.

Peter's colour returned and Susan patted him reassuringly on the back, almost as if, Lucy gulped in a breath, she knew his fears. She chewed on her lower lip with reflection as the parade turned into the rear yard stables.

They dined in the large airy kitchen. There was home-made chicken soup, followed by grilled trout although the children elected to have her special fish pie instead, and then a summer pudding which tasted divine. Susan had thought of everything. Lucy was most impressed, but not as much as Peter, who loved food, wherever it came from. Nestling in the afterglow of good food and splendid wine, for Peter had brought over a couple of bottles of Soave, they settled themselves back on the terrace for coffee.

While the children made daisy chains down in the nearby meadow they watched the sailing boats skim the lake, for the breeze was picking up, yet the terrace sheltered them from the slight chill in the air.

'We must have you both over to the cottage,' Peter suggested, glowing with wine and a good feed.

'We could do a picnic lunch and take it up the fells,' Lucy suggested, not yet relishing the competition from Susan's culinary skills. 'I'm afraid it'll be a simpler meal than this.'

'I've got a better idea,' Susan offered. 'You're all on holiday and I've got a freezer groaning with goodies, why don't I bring over a hamper and we'll take ourselves off for a ramble? It could be good fun if the weather holds.'

'And if it doesn't, then we'll stay indoors and eat it inside our little place,' Peter stated with determination. 'We could even play Monopoly. We had a great game the other night – before the squire knocked on the door, of course.' Lucy frowned with annoyance. 'I mean the owner of the place. Lord Grim.'

'Take no notice of him, Susan,' Lucy warned. 'He's rather biased about him.'

Susan looked puzzled for a second and then her face cleared and there was no mistaking the warmth in her voice. 'Joel's back home, then? I didn't know! He's rarely here now – but I suppose that's because of the nature of his profession.'

Peter scowled darkly. 'Away? Profession? I thought—'

'You thought what?'

'Well, he owns Monk Hall – and lots of land; he has horses, stock and a farm or two – I assumed—'

'Well, of course, yes, he is a landowner held in considerable esteem along these parts but he's made his name in a more complicated business than that, didn't you know?'

'Didn't we know what?' cut in Lucy with some impatience.

'He's a barrister.'

'A what?' Peter asked sharply.

'You heard me.'

'Crikey!' he managed to retort.

'No, we didn't know. He didn't tell us,' Lucy supplied.

'I'd expect that, I suppose.'

'Why do you say that?'

'He's not the type who would consider broadcasting his own importance. Besides, where it matters his good press precedes him. I used to think he was rather reserved. Have you seen him a lot while you've been staying here?'

'Er – no,' Lucy replied.

'One doesn't usually,' Peter added bluntly.

'He's been given splendid coverage over the last few months,' Susan remarked. 'Haven't you both heard about the Harrison conglomerate – and the big fraud case that has just been settled?'

'Vaguely—' Lucy thought back.

'Joel represented their case – he specializes in company law – has a formidable reputation, always a great demand for his services. In fact, he's represented some very big names over the last few years.'

Peter was astonished. 'Good heavens!'

'We didn't know.'

'I suppose his name wouldn't hit the headlines, company law doesn't sound sensational enough I suppose, but he's famously successful and well sought after for his expertise. He cleared the Harrison company – he was brilliant.'

'Spare me the details!' Peter looked as if he was getting bored with the subject.

Susan did not take the hint. 'I'm told he can be ruthless.'

'I can believe that.' His expression tightened.

'Don't you like him, Peter?' Susan asked.

'Not a lot!'

'Why? He's a lovely man. Don't you agree?' Susan looked at Lucy who found her skin tingling with heat, but was saved having to give an opinion for her hostess was eager to convey her own on the subject. 'It's a pity he's not married. Sometimes I think he must be rather lonely up there when he comes back home to enjoy a brief rest in between cases. He was very kind to me after Gerald died—'

'Oh yes?' Peter said darkly with new interest.

'The man has a very caring nature despite his hard-edged fame. Gerald was his tenant farmer. We were in serious financial difficulties – not that they came to light until after the accident; I suppose he was trying to keep the worries to himself.' She shrugged. 'When Manny Oliver brought the situation to Joel's attention he personally formulated a plan to get me over it. He waived the rent for the house until I'd sorted things out. I have the greatest respect for him.'

Peter looked askance. 'He doesn't seem to have much for me.'

'I think it's just a clash of personalities,' Lucy loyally explained.

Susan laughed huskily, and the sparkle in her eyes had a lot to do with her male guest as a little self-consciously she looked straight at him and offered the opinion, 'Joel and you are both distinctive in your own ways.'

On the road back, with the wind tangling their hair, Sophia leaned forward and put her arms around Lucy, clasping her small hands beneath her aunt's chin. The mountains towered all around them and, because the traffic was busy with tourists, Peter had no option but to take the road at a steady speed. Passing through Glenridding they could see it was bursting with strollers, basking in the summer sunshine and, down by the lake, families littered the bank shores, while Lucy watched a steamer cruise into the port to pick up passengers who wished to go down to Pooley Bridge which was situated at the opposite shore of the lake. Leaving the village the traffic picked up a little more speed as they skirted the shoreline, where the road became a series of curves and bends.

A Range Rover approached suddenly around one of the bends. Sophia recognized him first. She unclasped her hands and waved like mad. 'Look it's Mr Mortimer—' Her childish treble vibrated above Lucy's head and blotted out the roar of Peter's engine. 'Mr Mortimer, Mr Mortimer—' she called out. The Range Rover swept past without the driver taking his hands off the wheel. But he had seen them; Lucy had watched him. His face was unsmiling, perhaps he was concentrating on the traffic, maybe the sun was in his eyes and the bends were perilous, she had to admit. An ache grew deep inside her.

'Oh, he didn't notice us look. What a shame,' Sophia said, untroubled, unaware.

Lucy thought of those dreams. Then she considered the expression on his face as he drove past. It was hard, hostile. He wanted to ignore them. A sigh escaped her lips, and Sophia reclasped her hands around her neck but Lucy hardly noticed, the dreams were returning to tantalize. He had not ignored her then, and no mattter how hard she tried she could not stop indulging herself with those unbidden images of the night all the way back to the cottage. It helped to soften the rejection she had felt when he had sped past them with that unwelcoming look on his face.

Six

'Why not?' asked Peter. 'I thought you liked Susan.'

She finished packing thermos flasks into a holdall. 'I do,' Lucy said with fervour, 'but I'd rather miss out on this trip. Don't tell me you mind – I wouldn't believe it.'

'Sure you don't want to change your mind? I promise not to make you feel a gooseberry.'

She shook her head, her fiery curls swinging against her face. 'I want to ramble on my own today – I like my space too, remember?'

A noise disturbed them from above as his young daughter scuttled down the stairs to join them, dressed appropriately in jeans and shirt, with a sweater hanging from her arm. Lucy checked her over.

'Better bring down your jacket,' she advised. 'It's not so sunny today and there might be a shower; you can sling it in the back of your papa's car.' Even Sophia had Lucy using the word 'papa' now, yet Lucy rather liked it.

After they had gone, she drove down into the village to replenish supplies. As usual, when she passed the Hall she scanned the courtyard for signs of life. No response from the empty kitchen doorway: Winnie must be busy for she always glanced out and shared a few words with her, but Manny lifted his hand in a wave as he spotted her through his office window on the opposite side of the yard.

She recognized his tall, erect figure at once, dressed as usual in his country tweeds. She pressed the car horn then waved back at him and was rewarded by his honest smile. She had made his acquaintance four days ago, when she had encountered him in the yard where she had been about to lead Sophia through on their way to see the horses. Her first impression as he marched across the cobbled yard like a regimental officer on parade had appeared a little daunting. With his neat, grey moustache and carefully combed but thinning hair she could almost picture him barking out a command for them to halt. She quickly explained how the owner had permitted them to see his horses at any time. He knew all about them, of course, as he endorsed his employer's instructions, and even offered them a ride that very morning, to which Sophia was almost delirious with delight.

'Mr Mortimer's not here at the Hall now – in fact we don't expect him back for some length of time, but the young lad can take you both out – he's very reliable – the young lassie won't come to any harm.'

Acute disappointment made her almost breathless. He was absent, and not until then did she admit that a chance encounter had been the basis on which she had suggested they come up to see his horses. Now all thoughts of lingering vanished, leaving her disagreeably irritable. 'Oh no, but thanks all the same. We've already made our plans today and we've only half an hour to spare this morning.'

Sophia pouted in silence, but Manny shrugged, unoffended. 'Well any time, ma'am.'

'We'll come back tomorrow,' Sophia told him, looking up at Lucy. 'Can't we?' Her big eyes pleading her case.

'We'll see.' But they never did. There was Susan and Caroline and by now Sparky had been quickly conquered, so Sophia was not deprived too long of equestrian instruction. The attraction of Joel's horses soon diminished amid the more controllable and considerably smaller pony at the farm near Glenridding.

On the way back with fresh bread and the tabloid dailies she slowed to a halt as Manny strode out of his office.

'Good morning, ma'am,' he greeted. She loved the way he called her that, it endeared him to her; he made her sound so quaint and biddable, when if he only knew she was far from such a description. Although she repeatedly invited him to use her Christian name he preferred 'ma'am'. She had not the heart to discourage him. 'Mr Elliot and the little girl left early. Are you on your own today?'

'By choice,' Lucy explained. 'I thought I'd hike it to the top of the fell today.'

'There's a lake right up on top. Interesting to see, but don't think of a swim – it's dangerous. Very deep. Lots of weed.'

'A lake, eh? I'll do that.'

'Watch the weather, the forecast isn't good. And it can change as sudden as a lightning bolt.'

'I will. Thanks. Is Mr Mortimer back yet?' She managed all in one breath, trying to keep it light.

'Why?' Concern flashed across his face. 'Do you need to see him, ma'am?'

'No, no, I just haven't seen him around, you know.'

'He's still away – holidaying in the South of France with friends. I don't expect him here for some time.'

'Oh!' She started up the engine, eager to go, knowing the heat was suffusing her cheeks, and soon Manny would know she was not unaffected when mentioning his employer, no matter how casual she tried to make it sound.

She set off up the fell not long after. The woodland was more extensive than she realized as she walked through at a leisurely pace, her footsteps quiet on the packed layers of pine needles. Great clumps of fern cascaded gracefully under the tall trees. The quiet was eerie and a twig snapped suddenly some distance away which made her swing round sharply, trying to identify the noise; there was nothing she could see but she heard the soft scampering of a small animal as it bounded ahead out of her way. The feeling of eeriness gradually dissipated and, as she ventured along her route, the charm of the forest took over.

She supposed she should have hired some walking boots down at the nearby outdoor centre, slipping a little in her old Reebok boots where the track roughened when she emerged from the woods. She readjusted the rucksack on her back and pressed on, her skin clammy with perspiration, glad that she wore only a sleeveless green vest and shorts. She did not really plan to walk miles, and it had not seemed so far to reach the top.

Appearances, she judged, a lot later, could be very deceptive. Moorland now lay all around her, bleak, windswept, barren-looking even – until her eyes began to really notice it, for she spotted a group of partridges in the distance and later a startled moorhen took flight from only feet away, which nearly made her jump out of her skin. Enormous-looking bumble bees commuted across from the heather to gorse, far too industriously busy to take note of one lone walker.

She welcomed the breeze; she was so hot with the climb and her calves ached with the steadily punishing exercise. Walking long distances had not been on her agenda for some time, and driving a car had made her decidedly lazy, which had not helped any kind of fitness programme. Walking up here was anything but easy, she decided; it was steep, she slipped frequently and her breathing was getting rather ragged as she progressed upwards.

She reached the small lake an hour later. The climb was worth it, she considered, glancing keenly around her. Dragonflies hovered a few feet above the surface then dipped and skimmed across, their beautiful wings shimmering elusively like jewels moving to catch the light. It looked deliciously cool; she would have longed to have stripped off and slipped her unclothed body into its smooth, undisturbed surface and felt the heat evaporate from her hot flesh, but, mindful of Manny's advice, she merely prised off her boots and socks from swollen but thankfully unsore feet and paddled near the edge. She sucked in her breath sharply. The water was freezing! She slipped several times into its soggy depths, alerted to the fact that there was hardly any shallow shelving, so she moved cautiously back to the bank and, when she pulled out her feet, they were oozing with mud.

'Ugh!' she muttered, cleaning most of it off by dipping first one foot and then the other across the shallowest part until she judged they were relatively clean. Nonetheless, her toes tingled with numbness, yet it felt so good she still felt tempted to submerge herself. Further along the bank a choir of grasshoppers chirred spasmodically, abruptly stopping as she approached and continuing again as soon as she passed. She watched them with fascination as they leaped out of her way then settled almost indistinguishable against the grass. It was then she looked up and saw the warning notice not to bathe. She could almost picture Manny's face shaking his head and wagging one finger at her.

She shrugged, defeated, and turned for a grassy clump, retrieving her rucksack where she had dropped it earlier and sank down to rest before even thinking about turning back. By now the heat of the day was getting to her; there were clouds, but when the sun broke it was scorching. She slipped on her sunglasses to gaze around, but the heat sent shimmers up from the valley, yet directly across there was a breathtaking vista of craggy mountain tops, of crazily tilted trails etched into their sides. She spotted two climbers moving slowly upwards on the neighbouring fellside, and waved, feeling foolish when no wave was returned, but then, they had probably not even seen her, and distracting them like that might not be the wisest thing to do, she realized, dropping her hand and sinking back on to the short, stubble of grass.

She groped for her rucksack and bundled it under her head and presently, a culmination of the sun's warmth, coupled with the exhaustion of reaching the lake took its toll of her and she felt her eyelids getting heavier and her limbs sinking further into the ground. As a consequence she happily allowed herself to doze off.

The birds brought her back to consciousness, the raucous sound of their staccato alarms broke through her indolence. When she opened her eyes, she had no need of her sunglasses, indeed they had slipped off the bridge of her nose to nestle down on her vest front. But the gunmetal blanket of sky above her head, and the goose pimples that raised her flesh, gave an ominous testimony that she should move downhill soon, before the weather got worse.

Manny had warned her, often enough, never to take anything for granted when up on the high ground. It could change so suddenly, and without warning. Now she was learning the hard way.

She scrambled around looking for her boots and socks. The lake looked leaden and dull and, without the sunlight skimming its surface, a lot less inviting. At least walking at a brisk pace on the way back weighed slightly in her favour. It was dry, although, looking across to the adjacent mountain-top, or rather, where its summit should have been, for being higher than her level it was enveloped in mist, and the climbers to whom she had earlier waved were no longer visible in its shrouded cape, Lucy knew she had better move fast. The mist would very quickly sweep over in her direction and, as she watched, bringing a sudden frown across her brow, the wind quickened and fingers of cloud were already journeying across towards her. Without hesitation she settled the rucksack back on her shoulders and advanced down.

The rain was a fine drizzle at first, more the mist catching up with her than anything else, she decided, skidding now and then on the wet grass, cursing with increasing frequency the rubber soles of her boots which did not give any grip on the treacherous slopes. She could hardly believe how quickly the lowering mist caught up with her. Manny's dire warnings returned to fret her thoughts; how people could easily lose their sense of direction and trail the fell in ever-decreasing circles until, exhausted and confused, they perished, stranded with injuries and their bodies succumbing to the cold. This was summer, not the depths of a frozen winter where it was easy to imagine a numbing coldness could disarm the fittest of people. And she had not yet lost her way, despite the mist closing in, despite the weariness making her limbs tremble and her muscles rebel.

She was still a long way from safety. Her goal was the woods; it had taken her the best part of an hour to get through them, and she was on the wrong side from home, but it would at least make shelter, for the rain came down in earnest now, and her hair clung to her skull, while water dripped steadily down her clothes. It no longer mattered about the brevity of her shorts – jeans or leggings would have been similarly saturated. She should have carried a pack of waterproofs in the rucksack, that would have been the sensible thing to do, she thought with irritation. She had a towel in her rucksack, which she had intended to use after dipping her toes in the lake, but the sun had dried her skin instead and it hardly seemed appropriate now to wrap it around her head. Nothing seemed appropriate she thought wildly, slipping and sliding on a particularly tricky outcrop before stumbling blindly over a small boulder which brought a sharp cry of alarm from her lips, knowing that to wrench an ankle at this point in time would seem the most singularly inappropriate of them all....

She was tired, more tired than she could ever have imagined herself to be. Her legs ached, the muscles in her thighs and calves trembled with fatigue. She was almost on the verge of tears, holding them back with gritted determination. She had to go on, downwards, slowly, slithering each step inch by tortuous inch. She heard a voice calling her name and kept on moving, wildly aware that she was beginning to hallucinate and imagine his voice of all people.

'Lucy? Lucy, please God, answer me. Tell me you can hear me.'

She could not believe it.

'Lucy!'

It was him. Her breath was ragged, escaping in short vaporous bursts after her near tumble. Water dripped from the edge of her nose and she sniffed hard before attempting to shout back, a little hoarse at first but gathering strength when she distinctly heard his cry of triumph. 'Thank God,' she heard him reply. 'Keep shouting, keep talking to me – I'm moving up your way.'

Slowly through the shadowy landscape she watched his shape emerge. She laughed without humour, her thoughts still chaotic, bordering on to panic. How appropriate that it should be Joel, especially as it was raining. She was still smiling absurdly when he reached her but his expression was less than reassuring.

Needless to say her first words on sight of him were appropriately absurd. 'You're supposed to be in France.'

'France palled.'

'So soon?' She stiffened, then sneezed, hunting for her handkerchief.

He supplied her with a very large, white, dry one. 'You know why.'

She blew her nose then clutched the handkerchief and stared at him. She kept her response light. 'We really shouldn't keep meeting like this.'

'We really shouldn't be meeting at all,' he snapped back, the scowl staying on his face. She stared at his angry face. What did he mean, she wondered?

'Come on.' He took her arm and gasped. 'Oh hell, you're freezing!' But she felt wonderfully warm all of a sudden knowing he was there, by her side, knowing she was out of danger, realizing just how threatening that flight down the fell had really felt. Now she let her fears swamp over her, the pent-up worry erupted in a cascade of abject weakness which made her knees sag, and Joel had to hold her firmly, shaking her a little, and making her stand upright again.

'Don't go out on me now, woman. Here—' He wrenched off his waxed jacket and hung it over her shoulders. 'Lucy, do as I say and help me.' She stood like a rag doll, her mind too numb to think, her limbs simply could not operate. 'For goodness sake!' He thrust her arms into the sleeves and pulled it around her. The jacket swamped her shivering, drenched frame, but within seconds she could already feel the beginnings of warmth seep through her body.

'Thanks, Joel,' she muttered through chattering teeth and sniffed loudly, searching in the pocket of her shorts for his handkerchief. Then the rain increased with a sudden, violent downpour.

'We need to get out of this and find immediate shelter or you'll freeze,' he warned guiding her on down the fell. 'There should be the shepherd's hut nearby – we can't be far from it.'

He seemed to be certain of his directions, but Lucy blindly followed him, slithering now and again so that Joel held her firmly by the hand after that. She trudged obediently by his side, trying to keep up with his punishing pace. It seemed a good while before they found it, and by then, his hand felt as icily cold, but he maintained a firm hold of hers.

The hut was a squat stone building; large stone slabs sloped down on the roof where mosses greedily took over most of it, and on one side rose a stubby looking chimney. The door was sound and solid enough, and although the glass panes had long since been knocked out there were wooden boards nailed across the window to keep the worst of the elements at bay. 'It's years since I wandered into here,' Joel mentioned, testing the latch on the door and letting it swing open. 'Not since I was a boy.'

Inside it was very dark once Joel had shut the door. Their eyes accustomed themselves to the gloom. The only means of natural light filtered through the wooden boards that were nailed across the window frame. She watched him feel his way around to the small pot-bellied iron stove and kneeling down he began to search around it for kindling. He lifted up the lid and exclaimed his satisfaction. 'Good old Andrew – always prepared.' His hands groped across to some sort of wall shelf. Lucy watched him withdraw a box of matches and start the fire in the stove. The matches kept going out before he could get the thing going and he cursed the damp and his own clumsiness as he dropped the box, which spilled its contents all over the dusty floor. Lucy got down on her knees and groped for matches.

Presently flames caught, lighting up the interior of the hut. The flames licked hungrily through the kindling, and Joel began to feed the fire with small logs that Lucy could now discern in a small shadowy pile in the corner. 'That's better,' he said, standing up and watching the glow from the top of the boiler, his features thrown into a devilish light by the busy firelight.

Lucy swallowed hard and looked away, a small knot of emotion tugged deep inside her. He saw the movement. 'What's the matter?'

She shook her head, her hair tumbling in tight wet curls over her face. 'Nothing,' she mumbled, still dumbfounded at the feeling tearing away inside her.

'Are you unwell?'

'No – no, I'm fine. Don't worry.'

The flames roared inside the boiler, and she shuffled across to feel its heat. Her fingers tingled with a warmth which felt almost painful as she stretched out her hands. He moved, unbuttoning his shirt and tugging it off. She caught her breath, her heart pounded so heavily she felt sure she must be shaking with its effort. 'What – what are you doing?' she asked in a rather bemused voice.

'What do you think I'm doing?' His eyes were

dark pools against his hard face. 'I suggest you do the same – if you want to avoid a chill.'

Lucy slowly began to unbutton his coat.

Seven

The hut was small enough for the stove to do its work. Lucy found a hook behind the door and hung his jacket over it, watching the drips gather on the floor beneath it and wrinkling her nose as the pungent smell of animals filled her nostrils when warmth enveloped the place.

He noticed, his voice jocose. 'Sheep.'

'Sheep?' she repeated, wrinkling her nose even more.

'Andrew uses this place sometimes, not usually at this time of the year. In the wintry weather it comes in handy for him. Lambing can start unseasonally early sometimes.'

'You mean he stays here,' – staring around her in disbelief – 'Sleeps here?'

'If he has to – and it has been known.'

'Ugh!'

'His flock would have been grateful for his ministrations at the time—'

'I suppose we should feel grateful too – while the tempest roars outside.'

He smiled. 'We'll both smell pretty high if we have to remain for some while here.' She managed a small laugh, but the idea of spending some time here, alone with him – she did not want to think about that. 'At least,' he continued on a more serious note, 'you had the good sense to come down from the top with full haste.'

'The climb knocked me out – I simply fell asleep. It was so peaceful up there.'

'I know. I go there too – when I want to think.'

'Oh!'

'Sometimes, when I'm home. Have you got a sweater in your rucksack?' His eyes swept over her. 'You're pretty well soaked through as well.'

The T-shirt was revealing enough, she had already discovered that, and she also noticed he had no intention of averting his gaze. His eyes were bold, when she chanced a quick glance at him. The fact that he stood naked to the waist was disconcerting enough, for when he had shrugged out of his sodden shirt she had felt the heat impact her stomach and had to look away from him. She had been trying to do that ever since. She scrambled over to the rucksack and busied herself opening it. 'Manny said you were in France – on holiday.'

'Oh! You've been asking Manny about me?'

'I just wondered, as I hadn't seen you about – that's all.' Her fingers were suddenly clumsy, but she bent to her task. 'He – he thought you might stay there for some time.'

'I told you – it palled.'

'Where were you staying?'

'With friends – at their home in Cap Ferrat. It was a large house party. They invite me often but I don't always take them up on it.'

'Why? Does it depend upon the company?'

'Sometimes – sometimes not.'

She thought of them, wealthy socialites pursuing

the pleasures of that area. She thought of the women, elegant, sophisticated – desirable. She thought of him with them and now here he was with her, in this dirty, evil-smelling place. 'Lucky for me, I suppose – that you came back.'

'Why do you say that?' The lightness had gone now, instead he was sharp.

'Well, I would have been soaked – and probably lost. Goodness knows what might have happened.'

'You probably would have made your way back eventually. You were down far enough not to suffer too much from exposure,' he answered drily.

She looked up then. 'I'm trying to say thank you.'

His eyes were keen, as he answered quietly, 'I don't want it.'

Her fingers were feverish inside the rucksack now. The inflection of his voice, the softening of his words were wreaking havoc inside her. The warmth threatened the pit of her gut; she struggled to ignore it. Her fingers found the cotton material. She drew out the sweater. 'I forgot about this,' she said, without turning around.

She hoped he might turn his back, for she was pulling the wet top away from her torso. She took her time, so that he could tactfully turn away, and dropped it on to the floor. She glanced over. Joel was busy refuelling the stove. She felt very self-conscious as she dropped the sweater over her, glad to feel something dry on her skin for a change, ruefully dismissing her shorts. They would have to stay. Feeling more at an advantage she turned and stood up just as he did, and moved towards the greedy flames that shot above the stove top. He dropped the lid and turned. The sound of the roar of the fire in the belly of the stove filled the silence inside the hut, while above them on the stone slabbed roof, the rain drummed ceaselessly down. Their confinement seemed more pronounced because of it. Despite the awful smell of his sheep, there was a distinct cosiness, sheltering here, in the small stone building, with just him for company, and the busy flames that roared inside the stove.

'I feel much better now,' she said, deliberately avoiding any response to his last comment.

The silence lay heavily between them. He was standing by the stove watching her; his broad chest gleamed against the poor light. He had very fine body hair, darker than the pale brown colour which glistened slickly against his head. Her eyes darted away from the challenge in his, but they could not avoid him. The place was too small, and with him inside it, she found herself somewhat breathless. Not that he seemed to be having any difficulty with his breathing, she observed, sensitive to the atmosphere around them; there was no tell-tale tension cording his neck, or an agitated motion beneath his rib-cage.

Then why couldn't she relax?

It was impossible not to study him, her eyes were drawn, irresistibly attracted. His muscles gleamed, and her eyes clung to his finely tuned body, admiring it, fascinated, running her gaze down the sculptured lines of his shoulders, down past his upper arms, seeing the strength of his forearms as he suddenly turned sideways and busied himself adjusting the stove lid. She felt the tension ebb a little, while she admired the slender curve of his fingers as he shut it firmly down. The fine body hair stood away from his flesh, and she shivered, watching him, the warmth knotting her insides into a delightful, all-enveloping response.

He spoke suddenly, when she least expected it, once again engaging that tension she tried so hard to stifle within herself, causing it to vortex giddily inside her head when she realized what he was beginning to say. 'I don't want anything from you, Lucy. I think it wiser to feel that way, don't you?'

She bent her head and looked down to the floor. 'That – that's up to you.'

'I'm trying very hard to do that.'

The tension won. She could bear it no longer. 'Then why is it that you always seem to be rescuing me from awkward situations? Look, maybe I should get out of here and – keep out of your way—' Already she was turning, gathering her rucksack, but he was quick too, moving toward the door, barring her way.

His words were missiles well on target. 'My common sense says I should have stayed in France.' That was enough for her to attempt to push past him but his hand firmly held the door in place, stopping her. 'I'm sorry.' He sounded contrite. 'Forget that. You can't go yet – it's still pouring out there. Stay here – with me.'

She laughed softly, out of sheer nervousness. What was he doing? What was he saying? It steered them into an intimacy she had been trying to evade ever since he had brought her into this place. Now she began to grasp the full force of his reluctance, he was fighting every nuance of their attraction, hating it, driving himself to make her go, the awful truth of it stared her plainly in the face. His voice was sharp again, almost cold. 'Don't do that. This is not a laughing matter.'

There was an awkward silence. They were both ill at ease with each other, the tension filling the space between them became almost tangible until Lucy could hardly bear it. She had to do something to diffuse the situation, but there was nowhere to look now but at him. His face was strained, his blue eyes troubled. Raindrops ran down off his hair into his neck, making tiny rivulets down his chest. She turned back into the room, clutching the rucksack against her, then her fingers dug deep inside it and encountered the towel. She had completely forgotten about that until now, including it with the hope that she might have been able to take a dip in the lake. At least she had something to do, something to take their minds off what was happening.

She drew it out and moved towards him, dropped the rucksack to the ground. She held out the towel in front of her, making her movements quick, forceful, deliberate, doing anything to counteract that awful tension. With a mood of desperation she knew she had to dispel it somehow. She thrust the towel at him, intending that he take it to wipe himself dry.

'Here – dry yourself, your hair's soaking.'

She felt his hand, firm on hers above the towelling. 'Thanks, but yours is too, and it's a heck of a lot longer than mine.'

She made an attempt to stop him, his fingers curled around the towel and tangled themselves in her tight curls. She had made her own dilemma. The pressure was light but firm, she tilted her chin upwards, the stroking movements were pleasant and her intentions were soon thwarted. What was

wrong with this, she thought to herself? It was nice.
It was more than nice – and he was only trying to
help. Wasn't he?

She was becoming uptight for nothing. The
reflection made it much easier for her to relax. 'I
like that,' she murmured, her eyelids closing.

Joel made no reply, but the slow movements of
his hands continued. At first she meant it. It
soothed her, and he was making a practical effort.
Her hair was wet. He took his time. She liked it,
making no effort to stop him now. The more he
did it, the more she enjoyed those soft, rubbing
movements against her scalp. It was soothing. Her
eyelids lowered with a languorous heaviness. It
ebbed the knots of tension completely from her.
She forgot about what he had said. It no longer
seemed significant.

But then it changed, so subtly, before she could
stop things getting out of control. *Her* control, she
amended. Now they were. His hands, the touch of
his fingers upon her hair through the thickness of
the towel were enough. Her scalp tingled; her
spine felt feathers of reaction chasing down its
length; the warmth in her stomach expanded. Lucy
felt her control spiralling, sliding down into an
uncontrollable dizzy delight. *He* was the manipula-
tor and she was lost. It felt too good. She no longer
fought it. It felt wonderful.

He broke the silence. 'It's almost dry.'

'Mmm! Is it?' she said in a drowsily vague voice,
her head turned slowly against the movements of
his hand, she forgot all about self-control.

'You have beautiful hair—' His voice was
softening, she could feel his breath lightly across
her brow.

'Your hands feel wonderful,' she murmured.

He shook her a little, and it brought her against him, as her hands involuntarily shot forward to balance herself and encountered his chest. She caught her breath, while those traitorous fingers curled then uncurled against him. Had she not wanted to trail her fingers like this – ever since he had shrugged out of that shirt?

He let her.

Where was his reluctance now, she wondered without remorse? She could feel the steady pounding of his heart beneath her palm. It quickened as soon as her exploration began. His breast was firm, the hair-roughened skin was warm, warmer than she expected, growing with heat in fact as her touch lingered across him, languidly watching him beneath the sweep of her lashes, noting the way he caught his breath as the tips of her fingers brushed across the tautness of his nipple. His hand caught hers, stopping her, while the towel slid from her hair on to her shoulders.

He was rigid with tension now, she could feel that. His muscles rippled beneath her free hand as it roamed slowly upwards into the curve of his neck, feeling the strength of him as her fingers slid across his broad shoulders, acknowledging that every centimetre of him felt her touch and responded. His fingers moved over her captured hand, entwining with hers, lifting it almost to his mouth.

She watched him, waiting, her breath sharp, irregular, while her raised palm tingled with anticipation. Her lips were dry, she ran the tip of her tongue lightly across them, his dark eyes noting the movement. He bent his head slightly, she could feel his breath feathering the palm of her hand, his fingers were burning hers, yet she had no plans to pull them away from his. He seemed suddenly hesitant.

She was frantic. 'What's wrong?'

There were long painful moments before he responded. His words came as a complete surprise. 'This is wrong.'

'Why?'

'Because I want you.' His fingers tightened over hers. She sensed him battling with his own emotions. His words were tortured, given huskily. 'I want you too much.'

'I can handle that,' she murmured, her mouth curved into a soft smile. She stroked his neck. 'You're such a cautious man, Joel.'

'Because I know that I shouldn't get involved with you. I don't want to get involved.'

She gasped. Stunned. Her eyes filled with pain. 'You want me – but you don't want to get involved!'

'But I am now, aren't I – despite everything!' She was squirming from his hold now, but he clasped her hand tighter, 'I don't want to hurt you and if we—'

The towel slid to the floor as she tried to move quickly backwards away from him, but he followed her instead, still holding her hand.

'Let go of me – let go.' The soles of her Reeboks were wet and they skidded on the floor, then became entangled with the towel while she struggled with him until eventually she felt herself slowly losing her balance. There was nothing she could do to save herself.

His arms came fully around her, pulling her into

him. Her head turned into his nakedness, and her mouth was pressed against his heated flesh. She turned her cheek against his firm chest, no longer struggling, not wanting to, for one hand supported her back while his other threaded into her hair, urging her to stay. This was not the time to dissemble her emotions and it was far too late for Joel to deny involvement. He was involved, just as she was. He could no more move away from her than she from him. Their body language gave it all away.

In the dimness his face turned to hers. Their eyes locked, holding each other with the sheer hunger that gleamed like an inner light that could not be anything other than raw passion. His fingers cupped her chin, she moved willingly, eagerly, ready for him. Her eyes blazed with defiance into his – let him deny his involvement now! Joel lowered his head and kissed her deeply. It was almost savage in its intensity, as if he had wanted to do so for too long. She had not expected that, it alarmed her but it did not make her want to draw away.

He freed her mouth after that first heady kiss. Her lips felt raw and his features twisted with an inner torment. 'I was too rough!'

'No!'

'You haunt me, Lucy – I can't get you out of my mind but you know that. I tried to stay away but the image of you here – on my land – nearby – I couldn't keep away. I had to come back – just to see—' He stopped abruptly.

'To see what?'

'To see if this was all in my imagination. To settle it in my mind. Once and for all.' He traced her jawline with the tip of one forefinger, 'I called at the cottage. Then Manny said you were up here – alone. I worried myself sick knowing the weather was worsening. I was praying you were already coming back down when the mists lowered. I couldn't stop myself coming out to find you, cursing your inclination to walk up there – cursing our foul weather!'

'It got us here – together.'

'Yes.' His breath came urgently, and his hands were covering her once again, bringing her closer. 'As if it was meant to be,' he whispered as his mouth lowered over hers. 'And now I know – we both know – and dear Lucy, I can't stop this happening now!'

Her mouth sought his. 'Why stop?'

His lips were tender, producing an instant response from her. The tenderness did not last, it could not when so much rawness flared between them. She was as ardent in her kisses as he, their lips clinging, moving, tongues drawing an exquisite tangle of pleasure as they explored each other. When their gazes locked, Lucy felt as if her insides were melting.

He put her away from him. He needed to draw back. His voice shook. 'I'll feed the stove. It's so dark in here.'

She watched him, hugging her arms around herself, not with the cold, but she was trembling all the same, knowing he was going to come to her and take her into his arms once again. Then suddenly she listened, knowing something was different. The silence hit her. 'It's stopped raining,' she realized, blurting her thoughts aloud.

Joel looked up from his task, watching the flames

leap around the wood with vigour. 'So it has.' He stared at her across the room. 'We could go back, I suppose.'

She smiled, saying softly, 'Not yet.'

'No,' he agreed, moving back towards her.

She was much bolder this time. It excited him. She liked that too, seeing his pleasure, watching him catch his breath when her hands explored him, watching that burning intensity in his eyes when he stared down at her in a delighted surprise, then surprising her by his strength when he caught her against him. His body was waiting for her, while his hands caught the fullness of her breasts and made her forget everything, apart from his hands and mouth, his lips and tongue, and the soft words of love-making that emerged from his throat, husky, intoxicating words that she tried to match, overwhelmed now as they clasped themselves closely together.

'I want to be inside you – I want to possess you completely. You know that?' His hands reached for her waistband tugging at the button, impatient with the damp material that stuck stubbornly against her skin.

She was eager, helping, her lower body burning with the throbbing heat that raced crazily out of control within her, while her mouth clung to his body, pressing small, exploratory kisses across his shoulders, down his chest. Her words came out in one breathless rush of longing. 'I want to love you, Joel. Do you want to love me?'

He laughed huskily, his weight moving into her. 'You know how I'm feeling.' His arousal pressed impatiently against her loins.

'Tell me, Joel. Say it to me now.'

His hands began to peel down her damp shorts, his fingers lingering on the curve of her hip, sliding greedily down the side of her buttock. 'You know I want to make love to you – you've known it long before now. You knew it the night I brought you up to the Hall. I saw this sexy young woman scowling at me in the rain. I was lost. I wanted you then. I stood on the brakes so hard I nearly went into the hedge, I was so impatient to turn around and drive back, so anxious that you might make off. You stepped out into the road. I was doubly convinced. Then in the courtyard when I held you for the first time – I felt like a man who had taken too heady a drink. You must have known then.'

'Did I? We'd only just met.'

His teeth gleamed in the dimness. 'It wasn't just a figment of my imagination. Your face is very expressive.'

'You make me shameless!' She laughed. 'But it's true. It was the start of it. My desire for you.'

'Let's move over near the stove,' he suggested, drawing her towards the light. 'I want to see you when we make love together.'

'I might be shy,' she teased.

He laughed. 'I'll make you totally and indescribably immodest!'

He left her, reaching for his coat from the door hook and bringing it over with him. He laid it down on the floor, the dry part facing upwards and reached for her at the same time, his arms reassuring, his mouth possessing hers once again. Her blood began to race, knowing what he could do, feeling as she did for him. It had struck her here, in the hut, when they had entered, when the real truth had emerged. She had suspected all along, of course. Joel was right, the wanting had started the night they first met, but other emotions had drawn together the threads of those feelings, emerging slowly, day by day, knowing the loss of him, when he had gone away, feeling the misery of his absence, knowing a yearning for which she could not explain – yet, here, it was so clear. Sitting with him in his home, listening to him, talking with him, looking at him – learning all the time, acknowledging finally that this man was beginning to mean a great deal to her. Love for him overwhelmed her, obliterating from her thoughts his admission of reluctance. She would soon show him how easy it was for him to come to love her; she would make no restricting demands; he would soon learn he would never want to stay away from her again.

His kisses were slow and deliberate, while his hands moved over her, seeking her breasts from underneath the cotton sweater, pushing the material upwards so that Lucy half sat up, eager to discard the offending restrictions it imposed upon them, reluctantly dragging her mouth from his.

The door latch lifted and swung open. A draught of cold, damp air swept across them, and the light of a dingy afternoon filled the hut.

Joel jack-knifed upright. 'What the heck—?'

'Joel! Mr Mortimer! I'll be blowed!'

Lucy stared at the tall, lean figure of the man outlined in the doorway, while pulling down her sweater and groping with the zip of her shorts. She got herself decently put together as the man concentrated on Joel. It was Winnie's husband, the shepherd, she realized, scrambling lightly to her feet.

'I'm terribly sorry, sir, to barge in like this.' The shepherd meant it, still not daring to look at Lucy.

Joel slowly got to his feet. 'It's not your problem, Andrew. There's no need to apologize. We had to shelter from the wet for a while, that's all.' Lucy suppressed the sudden mirth of watching Joel acting as calm as anything, while the poor shepherd did not know what to do with himself.

'I saw the smoke, you see—'

Joel reached for his shirt, which was crumpled and damp, and began to drag it carelessly over him. 'I realize that. We were terribly wet – coming down that fell in the rain. It was imperative to dry off.'

'Yes, of course. sensible idea.'

Lucy felt the mirth filter away. The shepherd stared at her in total disbelief. 'I must apologize – er—'

'Lucy,' she supplied. 'That's OK,' she answered in a small voice, reaching for her rucksack and, gathering the towel, she plunged it into her rucksack, not daring to look at Joel. Something was wrong again. Totally wrong.

'I bumped into Manny. He told me you were looking – er – I've got the runabout down at the end of the trail, sir, that is if you and the, er, young lady are ready to want a lift back.'

Lucy felt sick. She had caught the look in Joel's face. It was filled with shame and regret. 'It would be better if we got down and out of these wet clothes, I expect.'

She looked away, disliking the tone, and pretended to check the straps on the rucksack. She felt anything but calm, but managed to keep her tone even and said, for the shepherd's benefit, 'I expect Peter and Sophia will be worried too.' The uneasy silence that followed alerted her to the fact that those words had not gone down very well. She stared at the shepherd. Did he harbour hostile feelings towards her brother too, like Joel obviously did? She sighed. Men could be so unpredictable.

Eight

She was very quiet. Peter noticed it. She pleaded a headache. He put it down to her soaking while out on the fell. He plied her with aspirin and hot lemon drinks and built up the fire and cosseted her until she felt mad with the distraction of it. She wanted to think. Be alone. She felt so confused.

All the way back on that slow, miserable drive down in the station wagon, with Joel at the wheel and she sitting alone in the back, behind the two men there had been a silence so thick with a tension she had not had the nerve to break. She had caught his eyes upon her a few times through the driving mirror. He had looked grim and angry and, she sensed with an awful precision, ashamed of himself.

'Don't you think it's time you drove over to Susan's to collect Sophia?' she suggested, flashing him a snappy look.

Peter glanced at his wristwatch. 'I should have made you come with us today.' His expression was mischievous. 'I'll bet Mortimer gave you a right old lecture about safety on the fells when he found you looking like a drowned cat.'

'He was too soaked to care.'

Peter smirked. 'Good. I hope he's snuffling into

his hot toddy right this minute looking as pathetic as you.'

She supposed he had meant to be humorous, but her spirits were too low. 'I'm really not interested in what the man is doing at this moment.'

'Oh?' He glanced over at her sharply. 'Don't tell me he really did give you a hard time?'

If she was not careful she was going to reveal the very thing she was trying to conceal. A primness soured her voice. 'I did not enjoy being soaked. I did not enjoy being stranded in a smelly shepherd hut and I certainly do not enjoy sitting here with the imminent onset of flu – or worse – while you pontificate about the safety of fell-walking.' She stuck out her tongue and glared at her brother.

Peter laughed. 'That's more like my old sister!'

Now that she had deflected his attention her tone was very persuasive. 'Go on over to Susan's. I'll be all right. I intend to go to bed – an early night will soon have me feeling my old self in the morning.'

After she heard the sound of his racer roar up the hill and set off to traverse the courtyard through the Hall, she delayed going upstairs and settled back on the sofa to relax and idly watch the flames of the fire roar and kindle up the chimney. She was in no mood for company – anyone's. The events of the day raced through her mind, bringing back that nagging undercurrent of unease.

Later, upstairs on her narrow bed, she pulled the quilt cover over her and curled into a foetal position and closed her eyes. Images of him filled her mind. Images of them together heated her blood. She moved restlessly to lie on her back and stare at the ceiling. An emptiness hollowed her insides until it ached.

If the shepherd had not disturbed them— She closed her eyes as if the shadows hurt them. She could still sense Joel's miasma of guilt. It had hung heavily in the close confines of the station wagon. So one of his employees had nearly stumbled upon them in the act of making love? What was so wrong about that, she kept asking herself over and over again? She could not believe his image as the owner of Monk Hall had suffered so greatly, or that he was worried too much over his dignity. Then what had made him act so distantly as they motored back down the fell track? She could not accept it was because they had been discovered. After all, the repercussions from it would cause no more than a few remarks to his wife maybe, bringing a quiet amusement between them in the privacy of their own home. Winnie and Andrew Heskett were loyal to him. They would exercise discretion. Besides, they were both consenting adults – and she had so wanted him to fall in love with her when she knew she was in love with him – but he *was* falling in love with her. Had he not cut short his stay with friends to come back and find her!

She walked up to the Hall the next morning, soon after breakfast, leaving the others to clear up in the kitchen. She had said she wanted a brisk walk to clear her head, relieved that neither wanted to come with her, for if they had she would have had to found an excuse to stop them. There was a purpose to her walk, she had thought of nothing else all through the night.

It was going to be hot. She was dressed for it, wearing the briefest of denim shorts with a white cotton top which she had gathered in a tight knot against the front of her waist and her bare feet were thrust into her scuffed trainers. As she reached the Hall she noticed the swallows; they swooped and soared around the yard. She encountered Winnie, moving across it with a basket filled with new-laid eggs. The older woman smiled and offered her some of them. Lucy shook her head and asked if Joel was about. Winnie looked extremely interested but Lucy deliberately acted offhand.

'He's not indoors. Do you want me to get him for you?'

'Well, not if he's—'

Winnie cut her off. 'He mentioned he'd be busy, mind you – he'll be out in the barn behind Mannie's office.'

Was Winnie trying to put her off? She wondered if her husband had recounted what he had seen. Most husbands would. She kept her voice light, 'I'll saunter round and have a quick word with him.'

Winnie looked very pensive as she replied, 'I'd better warn you – he's not in the best of moods.'

Lucy felt her spirits plunge. 'Isn't he?'

'Something's on his mind, I expect.'

'Oh!' Lucy's face flooded with colour. 'You mean it would be best if I didn't disturb him?'

Winnie shrugged, but her voice had a doomed air about it. 'I suppose that's up to you. I'll be in the kitchen if you want to share a coffee with me later on.'

Lucy's smile was tremulous. 'That would be nice.'

She knew where the barn was, slipping through the embrasure and glancing instinctively across the paddock. The grey lifted her head and whickered a greeting, the others, predictably stared at her with interest, then realizing she was not moving forwards to the fence but skirting the outer wall to reach the barn instead, they dropped their noses to graze, uninterested, their tails lashing out with regular irritation at the unwelcome attention from the flies.

Now that she was about to confront him, Lucy could feel a prickle of sweat erupt between her shoulder blades, and the cotton top clung uncomfortably against her skin. She pressed her palm against the bare skin beneath the centre knot of the cloth and fervently wished she had not encountered Winnie this morning. The older woman's attitude unnerved her.

The barn was enormous, ancient, built of weathered stone and with a sound pitched roof of stone slabs and, as she approached it, she was able to discern that one of the massive oak doors stood open. Her footwear made no sound on the grass, or on the track that she crossed to reach it. She looked inside. Her eyes took some moments to adjust to the gloom. Bales of hay were stacked against one entire wall. A Landrover was parked at the far end, where, she noticed beyond the dusty haze, a single door stood open.

A bird caught her attention, a house martin, flying with speed from one oak-timbered beam to the other, sunlight slashed through every available aperture, shafting between the evenly placed ventilator gaps across the upper part of the barn and flooding through the partially exposed entrance. The air was cooler inside, but only slightly, and it did nothing to alleviate her discomfort. Dust motes swirled in the shafts of light, and it was so quiet she thought Winnie must be mistaken. Joel was not inside.

Then the tranquillity ceased with the sound of a heavy metal object as it clattered with a ringing echo on to the ground. Her gaze sought the direction of sound, settling in the region of the parked Land-rover. She heard him curse, a sharp, succinct oath that he would never dream of saying if he had known she was standing nearby. She took a deep breath to calm the flutter of fresh nervousness and called out to him while she advanced across the barn floor.

A pair of denim-clad legs protruded from under-neath the vehicle. He slid out from it, exposing a white polo shirt which bore the recent evidence of his mechanical efforts as she noticed traces of grease across its front. He scowled up at her, levering himself up with his hands and discarded the span-ner he held into a tool box nearby.

'Did you want me for something?' His eyes lazily looked her over. 'Or are you merely passing the time of the day?'

'Winnie said you were busy.'

'As you can see – I am. Very.'

'Is that a statement?'

'Take it which ever way you will.' He selected a smaller spanner from the toolbox, glancing into it and away from her, so that the muscle working in his jaw caught her interest as he added, 'As long as you don't waste my time.'

'Oh don't give me that, Joel Mortimer,' she challenged with spirit. 'You're not in the courtroom now – or negotiating with a client – and yesterday, in the shepherd's hut, you obviously thought it time very well spent!'

He dropped the tool back into the box and glared at her. 'Wouldn't you think it best if we forget that?'

'Why?' Her temper exploded. 'Are you ashamed of yourself?'

He did not look away. 'Yes. I damn well am.'

'Don't demean it, Joel.'

'It would be better.'

'Don't you remember what you said?'

He bent his head and stared down at the ground. 'Regrettably, I recall everything very clearly.'

'Regrettably huh? What you said – what you did to me—'

His eyes swung back to lock with hers. 'Then forget it!'

'I can't be casual about it!'

'Look Lucy, I'm trying to be very discreet. I'm trying to be sensible, for goodness sake. Now I suggest that you don't attempt to make another issue out of it. I can keep out of your way – I realize I have to – now can't you do the same for me?'

She felt wounded. 'Is that what you want? I'm to avoid you?'

'Yes. It is.'

'It would seem that I've made a fool of myself.'

'No you haven't. I'm guilty of the mistake – I should have known better.'

'Don't patronize, Joel. I don't need that.'

'I wasn't trying to.'

'You're trying me!'

'Why did you have to come up here? You should have thought it out. I imagined I made it very clear to you yesterday. I tried to—'

'Yes you did. As I say – you're very trying.'

'Don't play on words, Lucy.'

'No – I suppose that's your forte, isn't it? Don't you like someone else playing you at your own game, Joel? You don't like being put on the spot – nor it seems do you like having to take the consequences for your actions.'

'You're a very lovely woman. I told you that.' She coloured, the heat spreading uncomfortably across her flesh. 'And I'm attracted. I told you that also.' He drew himself to his feet, and looked down at her. 'What else do you want of me?'

'I don't know, I suppose.'

'You suppose?'

'I could say that's why I came looking for you. I'm confused, Joel, and soon, very soon, in fact, I shall have to leave.'

'I know that.'

'Well? I don't know what to do – say – can't you help me out?'

'I am.'

'I don't understand.'

'Don't you, Lucy? I don't believe you're that naive.'

The flies droned around them, otherwise the stillness was deafening. She was totally confounded. His attitude, his demeanour, was baffling. He behaved as if there was a great restraint between them. A barrier of which she had no knowledge. He wanted her to leave him alone, he had made that plain enough. She supposed she should go, her logic told her to get out of the barn, but emotion held her back. She could not forget what had happened between them up on the fell yesterday. Something that had been growing steadily between them since they had met. That made her stay, only that gave her hope and her love had no pride.

So she lingered, searching her mind for new ways to resolve this unbearable situation between them. It was then she discovered that she need not say anything at all. Joel leaned back against the side of the vehicle, his eyes lazy, watching her. A sigh escaped his firm mouth as his gaze lingered. She knew he liked looking at her, that same darkening glance, the heat in his eyes, it was there, springing again, and she suspected he had not yet realized it. The blood began to pound in her veins, just like before, like the other times when he was watching her, when he was near – the attraction was heady.

'That's a fetching outfit,' she heard him say.

The softly spoken words disarmed her. She felt the strength in her limbs weakening. His voice encouraged it. There was a tautness about him; she could not define it specifically, but it was there, just looking at him, she knew it was there. Like a dangerous predator waiting to spring she thought with heightened imagination. Dangerous. Excited. He conveyed it to her without even moving, it emphasized his strength somehow, and she was not impervious to it either, in fact, her pulses were quickening at a rapid rate. Control slipped from her; she no longer wanted it, because she wanted him.

'Is it for my benefit, I wonder?'

'Benefit?'

'You've got good legs, I like looking at them – but then you know that – I liked looking at them when you stepped on to the road, remember?'

'What do you mean?'

'I told you about it yesterday. When you got out of the car that night. The night you ran out of fuel. If I hadn't been coming along then—'

'What the heck are you talking about, Joel?'

'I'm just trying to get my mind sorted out, Lucy, especially where you're concerned.'

The ideas converged. Unpalatable. Unpleasant. Was he saying he wished they had never met? How could she even want to love him on the basis of that? She licked against the sudden dryness of her lips. 'You want me to get out of your life. Out of here. Don't you?'

He sounded very careful as he answered. 'That would be a good idea. Yes.'

'You conduct's appalling. Do you know that?'

'Is it?' His look was sharp. 'What about yours, Lucy? You haven't exactly acted like a shrinking violet.'

'It's never been my style,' she snapped back, 'and if you don't like it you're living in the wrong country. I can look at my face in the mirror and not turn away. Can you?' Her lip curled; she was already moving away from him, avoiding contact, any contact. Why had she so desperately wanted to come to him? She must have been insane! Her eyes searched the place, trying to find an opening at the other end of the barn, the tears were too much, threatening, flooding. She dared not swallow, the restrictions in her throat worsened, but she dared not make a sound. The sob hovered, constrained tightly at the back of her throat. Where was the door? There must be another way out? Hadn't she noticed a door at the other end when she first entered?

'I'm sorry. I shouldn't have said that the way I did.' He was close, too close. He was right behind her. Following. She hurried, searching blindly for the door, the tears a thick wall blocking out vision.

She spotted a sharp shaft of light and made for it with haste, not seeing the straw bale until she fell awkwardly over it.

'Oh!' She righted herself with her hands, the straw rough against her palms.

'Lucy! Don't go like this,' he implored.

Who was he kidding? Her thoughts bounced; she felt wild, furious. Had he not just made his position perfectly clear? She hastened, moving for the door as if it meant impending doom if she did not make it.

She didn't. His hand caught her arm and swung her sharply back against him. 'I'm trying not to hurt you – but I know no other way to end it.'

Hysteria rose in her throat and she struggled, trying to pull herself away from him, but his hold was firm. 'Don't bother – I'm not dense. There's nothing to end – and you've made it perfectly clear that I'm' – she stumbled on the words, – 'I'm not wanted.'

She heard the rawness in him. 'But you are – you are – so desperately.'

She turned in his arms. 'I don't believe you, not after what you've said. It was cruel, Joel. I'll never forget it.' To her chagrin the tears spilled down her cheeks in a fresh humiliating flood. She shook her head and turned away.

His other hand fell on her shoulder, which prevented her from going further away from him. 'You're right, Lucy, I can't look at myself in the mirror especially when I should know better. Yet I see your anguish and feel exactly the same. Don't make me do this – it's better not—'

'Is it? For whom? You – or me?' His hands drew her around to face him.

His mouth was angry, hard, hotly exploring hers, turning her body into him, feeling her softness, ignoring her constraint, taking away her hands that attempted to stop him from his chest holding them instead, drawing them around his back, impelling her to embrace his body, while the movement brought them closer together.

Once there, she was trapped. And so was he. The anger went, her fury vanished, replaced by something infinitely more powerful. Beneath the thin cotton material she could feel the heat of his body and the heavy thud of his heartbeats, racing out of control, like hers. Her hands unclenched and she allowed her fingers to splay against him. Passion exploded, unchecked by either of them, building in intensity with each pressure of his mouth against hers, so that she was aware of every signal which her body encountered, from the demanding explorations of his kisses, to the slow, deliberate discoveries of his hands.

Her skin was burning, but then, as her fingertips slipped beneath his cotton shirt, tracing the smooth hardness slowly up the long line of his back, his felt on fire beneath her touch. He was tense, his muscles contracting as she stroked him with slow movements of pleasure. She knew he liked it, and that excited her even more. She gasped for breath as his mouth moved, and a moan escaped from her when he sought the soft vulnerable area against her neck, where beneath the skin, a pulse throbbed beneath the demands of his mouth.

He crushed her to him, the power in his hands holding her against him so that the tautness of his thighs and the hot pressure of his groin tormented her desire. She wanted more, her body craved a satisfaction that frustrated her. Her breasts ached for his caresses, and further down, her loins harboured a delightful sensation of expectancy, waiting for his possession. His hands moved to her shoulders and he pressed her downwards, his mouth reaching once again for hers. The barn floor was cool but dry and wisps of straw itched against her back, but there was a satisfaction in her eyes when he levered himself above her. There was none in his.

'This is what you came up for, isn't it?' His fingers tangled into the knotted cotton against her waist.

She felt him loosen her shirt, alarmed at the look in his eyes. She stopped his hands with her own, threading her fingers through his, but aware that the folds of the shirt had already dropped open. His eyes wandered, studying the pale honey-coloured swell of her breasts beneath the chaste whiteness of her underwear. His head moved downward and her breath quickened with panic. The look in his eyes bore no relation to what was happening between them. 'Wait—'

He looked up. 'You chose the time and the place. You wouldn't go away. I tried to warn you – and you know how to get to me, Lucy – you know how to do that so cleverly, and if this is really what you want why should I deny myself your pleasure, hmm?'

'Why are you looking at me like that?' Her voice was troubled, the hard expression on his face filled her with doubt. 'I thought—'

'You thought what?' Not waiting for an answer his mouth brushed the soft swell of her breast, and her body betrayed itself, the chemistry between them a tangible potency which vanquished her doubts.

'I thought you wanted me too.' She sighed as his lips searched the edges of her bra.

His voice was hard. 'I don't dare think at all.'

His kisses were fierce, catching her unprepared for them and unaware. His mood was unpredictable, one moment she was sure of him, and the next, when his body hardened while his hands curved around the smooth curve of her buttocks and his mouth dominated hers she felt a turmoil within him that she could not understand. All she wanted was to show him how much she loved him, and soon, very soon, she hoped Joel was going to be as frank with her about his feelings. For the moment, she could do nothing else but match his need with her own, and on the hard ground, with his long, lean body over hers, and with limbs entangled, and the quiet surrounding them, she felt cocooned in a private world of their own.

'Lucy—'

'Hmm! What?' The drone of insects hung heavily in the air around them.

'Get up.'

She laughed softly, more concerned with their sensual delights, then realized his weight was shifting from her. 'Joel! What's the matter?'

'Nothing. Just get up.'

Her arms urged him back to her. 'I don't want to – is someone coming?'

'No.'

His kisses left her drugged. She did not want to leave this world. Why was Joel making such a fuss when only seconds earlier they had been on the point of something deeper, much deeper, much more intimate than kissing and touching? Much more than that.

He was already levering himself away from her. She felt a lightness across her body and realized Joel was getting up off the ground. She looked up at him, his hand was stretched out for hers. Instinctively she took it with her own and felt herself hauled off the ground with some force.

'What's the matter?'

'You amaze me!'

Straw clung to both of them. She brushed it away from her shorts, and re-knotted her cotton top. Somehow standing together with that serious look on Joel's face, Lucy supposed he felt embarrassed; it was not exactly romantic trying to make love in such open surroundings. If she really considered it, she might feel exactly the same, but being near him and feeling as she did, embarrassment was the last thing on her agenda at this moment.

She attempted to lighten their situation. 'I suppose you don't want to feel compromised,' she suggested with some amusement, catching his eye as he brushed straw from his jeans. She expected he was trying to formulate a suggestion to go up to the house. His rooms would be private, very private, once they got past the hurdle of Winnie.

But then Winnie knew. Lucy smiled thinking about it. Winnie had realized what was going to happen for a long time. The thought did not worry her. Joel worried her more. The look on his face was even more serious. The whimsical notions began to dissipate. The doubts returned, haunting her mind. Torment invaded his taut features and he was looking at her with an awful forbidding expression on his face.

'I want you to leave Monk's Hall, Lucy, leave it and never come back again. You're not good for me. I know that. You should have known it all along. I want you, I don't deny it, but I can't love you. I won't love you – no matter how tempted you make me feel to do so.'

Nine

Winnie rattled her knuckles on the small square-paned window making Lucy start with fright. When she saw Lucy spin round to the sound she stared for some moments before speaking. Then she mouthed the words hastily, 'The kettle's boiling, dear. Come inside.'

'I can't!' Lucy's voice sounded shrill to her own ears, backing away from the window and Winnie's shrewd eyes, aware that there was nothing she could do or say to stem her curious scrutiny so, in consequence, turned to advance with haste across the courtyard, furtively glancing across to her right to see if Joel was following.

It seemed not. Nonetheless, she walked as quickly as she dared without commanding, at least she hoped it did not, undue interest, especially from Winnie, whose eyes she could almost feel boring two burning holes into her thinly clad back. She heard the deliberate summons as Winnie rapped again, this time more forcibly – or was it her vivid imagination? Lucy could not be sure – on the glass pane.

She turned around and spread out her hands in a gesture of helplessness, hoping the older woman could not discern just how upset she felt. 'I'm late,' she explained, shouting over to the motionless but expectant figure at the window, 'Peter and Sophia will be waiting – maybe I'll call by another time.'

Winnie hurriedly lifted the sash and loudly supplied her endorsement to that. 'Make sure you do,' and then, because she could not resist it, 'I warned you he was in a mood of sorts, but you wouldn't listen, I warned you he'd be difficult!' But Lucy was moving so fast she doubted the younger woman heard for she was already disappearing out of the courtyard to descend the track to the cottage. Winnie rammed down the sash so hard the glass rattled in the wooden frame, muttering with earnest vehemence under her breath, 'These modern women! I shall never understand them.'

Although she could not see them, for the meadow banked steeply up the rear of the cottage, Lucy could hear Peter and Sophia playing some kind of ball game there. The child was laughing, sounding so carefree and happy. She loved the way Sophia used the name 'Papa'. It had a precious ring to it – at long last she felt they were a real part of being a family again. It was imperative that she conceal the way she felt. She did not want their world disrupted. At least she could hold that part of her life intact. It was so important – so very dear – especially now.

She slid inside the cottage undetected, and upstairs stared at her image in the small wall mirror on her bedroom wall. Her woeful reflection did not surprise her. She felt bruised, beaten and battered, yet no physical blow had been dealt. The wounds were mental, and the punishment of it showed in her haggard, staring reflection.

There was grease on her cotton top she noted

dully, indistinct smears of it from Joel's polo shirt, she surmised. There was straw on the floor from her fingers. There was even streaks of grime on her cheeks where his fingers had touched her. She thought of him touching her. They had not cared then.

She felt soiled and unclean, not with the grime on her clothes, but the aftermath of his blunt statement. He wanted rid of her – out of his life, out of his system. She wondered if he would find it as easy as he thought. Lucy chewed on her lip with suppressed fury. How could she feel so much for him? How could she still feel this way? Even now! She supposed that was why it hurt so much.

She stripped off the offending garments and stuffed them out of sight into her holdall and, gathering her robe and soap bag, she headed along towards the shower. She took her time. The hot jets soothed her body, soaping the grime from her, shampooing the straw and the dust out of her hair, the cleansing motions a perfect catharsis to her emotional conflict. It was never going to be easy as that to erase him from her mind or her heart.

Sophia's girlish laughter drifted up the stairs, heralding their return from the meadow. Lucy lingered in the bathroom a little while longer. She was not ready yet. No one could disturb her there, if she kept the shower running with full power, not yet. When she had finished rinsing all the physical traces of him from her, when her heart ceased to pound with the dull ache of pain, leaving an empty void of the acceptance of it, she padded back in her bare feet to her room to pack.

She plucked out the hangers from the wardrobe and flung them on to the narrow bed then, picking up the garments that spilled on to a heap over the duvet, she dressed in the clothes she had arrived in when she had first come to meet Peter. It seemed like months ago – had so much happened in her life?

She glanced in the mirror with a practised eye. They made her feel feminine and in command, she supposed, yet it felt like she was putting on her armour, her protective image displayed so professionally – the short skirt, the smart tailored blazer, the application of just the right amount of make-up and the final touch – taking particular attention with her hair, dressing it in a red cloud of curls around her face. She might be wilting inside but no one was going to know about it. She reached across the dressing-table and clipped on a pair of square, bold, solid gold ear-rings.

Lucy stared at her reflection. No one could possibly suggest she was running away from here. She looked too composed and together, just the right image she decided that a fashion journalist should look. This was far from the wild-eyed woman who had fled in bitter humiliation from a dusty old barn. She forced the image from her mind and boldly sprayed on one of her favourite French and enormously expensive scents against her neck and inner wrists, then hoped the midges would give her a wide berth.

There was so much pent-up energy erupting inside her she had no option but to keep on the move. Doing that made thinking unnecessary, besides, what was there to talk about? Packing the rest of her stuff into the holdall did not take long, soon she would have to make her way downstairs and tell Peter and his daughter something. Not the real reason of course, but a good enough excuse to be returning so quickly and without warning to London.

In the end it was easier than she thought.

Sophia was busy stuffing the wild flowers she had picked in the meadow into a glass jar and arranging them on the dining-table, but Lucy's brother noticed the bulging holdall in her hand as soon as she clattered down the stairs on her very high-heeled court shoes. 'You're going back? So soon?'

'I have to. I hope you don't mind.'

His shoulders hunched as he dug his hands into the pockets of his jeans. 'You're bored, aren't you? I should have guessed yesterday when you said you wanted to walk up there alone. You bit my head off. You've been grumpy ever since.'

She did not like being reminded about that, but managed to conceal the fact by shaking her head, the curls flying wildly about her cheeks, dishevelling the carefully arranged tumble a little and jangling the ear-rings against her lobes. She readjusted the jewellery and scrunched the tendrils of hair back with her fingers. 'No, it's not that at all. I liked being here with you both.' Licking her glossed-up lips she continued on a more positive note. 'But I have to go back – I – I have to find a job, Peter. I can't just laze about forever. I have to earn my keep and I already have spent some time out of the action while holidaying in France remember? Coming up here and delaying work, although I didn't mind that especially when I was coming up to meet you, and—' She smiled with a rush of warmth at the child who looked a little crestfallen at the news. 'Meeting Sophia was not to be missed – but if I don't show my face and peddle my talents no one else will do it for me. Besides, I promised a colleague I'd get in touch with her soon.' The lie sounded so genuine she hated doing it. 'There's a features opening on her paper if I want it – but it won't wait for ever, you know how it is.'

Peter was convinced. 'OK – I understand – you should have mentioned this sooner.'

'I didn't want to spoil the visit. It's been good, hasn't it? Look, when you've had enough here I expect that you'll both come down and stay at the flat with me, won't you? I mean you and Sophia together.'

'Where do you live?' asked the child, who looked a little alarmed and insecure at the fact that she was so suddenly leaving them without warning.

Lucy's voice was full of reassurance. 'In London. I have an apartment there – you'll like it, darling. There's lots to do.'

'London's a very big place, isn't it?' She swivelled round to Peter and asked, 'Can we, Papa?'

Her brother looked doubtful. Lucy knew he wanted to remain here and spend some time with Susan. 'Next vacation, honey, there's not enough time to fit in staying there now. You go back to school at the beginning of next week.'

Lucy smiled at her niece. 'You can come and stay with me during half-term, if you like, that is if your papa can't make it over here. There's always a place with me.'

Her brother beamed with surprise. 'Would you? That would be wonderful.'

Lucy's voice was firm. 'I'll look forward to it.'

'I'll try and wangle leave for then and fly over for a few days and stay too.'

'Do your best,' his sister urged.

'But what about Caroline – and her mama?' Sophia looked agitated. 'You promised that we would be staying with them again soon too – and that would mean during my half-term, wouldn't it? We can't do both. There's not a lot of time during half-term.'

The very mention of anyone in this immediate vicinity made Lucy feel agitated but she managed a laugh, just for effect. 'I'll invite them down at the same time – how's that? I think Caroline might enjoy looking around the city with us. It would make a change from staying in the countryside.'

Peter had a better idea. 'Cities can be claustrophobic, Lucy. We both know that, we had to grow up there, remember? But Sophia has a point: you could come up here, I'm sure Susan wouldn't mind. She's already invited us to stay with them at their place anytime during school breaks and she's got plenty of room, she won't mind.'

The very thought of returning to this place made her head spin. Lucy became very quiet. So there was a hint of something deeper happening with her brother and the young widow across the lakeside. At least someone in the family was gaining happiness. She stared at her brother and diplomatically replied, 'I don't think I'll get that much free time if I find a new job – not so soon anyway.'

'There's no rush about it,' he brushed aside the problem. 'We can make definite arrangements later.' He was totally unaware of her turmoil.

She was certainly rushing her exit, she supposed.

They waved her off as she drove her little Renault up the track towards the Hall. Once they were out of sight she put her foot down, traversing *his* place was going to be the worst part. She wanted to see no one, no one at all. She drove through the courtyard with some speed, the car wheels bouncing on the cobbles.

She thought she saw the tall figure of Manny Oliver begin to rise up from his desk in his office as she swiftly shot a glance through his window but she was moving too quickly for him. At any other time she would have at least thrown a smile in his direction, but she was not able to summon one up for poor old Manny. Just leaving the cottage without a seeming care in the world had extinguished all her efforts; there was too much pressure on her to get out of this place.

If she had been spotted by Winnie she did not know what she would have done. Winnie would know she was leaving – and why. She speculated on Joel's return to the house and wondered what particular frame of mind he must have displayed. Winnie would have been waiting for him, she felt sure. She hoped the woman had been difficult. It afforded her a faint glimmer of satisfaction knowing that.

She steered the car out on to the road that took her down on to the public highway, breathing a sigh of relief that she was through the worst. She could not wait to shake this particular dust from out of her wheels. It irritated her sensibilities far too much for comfort.

In her eagerness for flight she was forced to slam on her brakes halfway down the steep track, for a trades' van was leisurely ambling its way up to the Hall. The mail van, she amended, smiling at the driver as she waited politely in the appropriate curve that afforded vehicles a decent passing place, glancing idly in her mirror when the red van drove past her. He seemed to take an age, thus increasing her impatience and sense of urgency. She glanced in her mirror to move off then something else caught her attention, causing her pulses to leap wildly in reaction to it. Her eyes were riveted not on the track, or the road below, but to her left, directly on the upper slopes of the moorland.

They emerged more clearly now that they had cleared the paddock enclosure. The rider on the grey horse was making speed, taking the fell without dropping pace. She knew who he was without taking a second look. He was still dressed in the jeans and polo shirt she had last seen him wearing earlier. The only difference was that he wore riding boots which accentuated the long length of his legs and from time to time he pressed his heels into the horse's side to change her step and pace as he changed direction and turned down the slope to make his way down the moorland. Then Joel was giving the mare her head. Her proud profile thrust forward in a rhythmical motion, her nostrils flaring with effort. Lucy's gaze swung back on to the rider. His hair streaked back against his beautifully proportioned head with the force of the wind against them, and his face was turned upwards to the elements, the hot sun against his face and bare arms. She could imagine the coolness of air as it rushed against him, almost as if he welcomed the feel of it against his skin, he looked strong and healthy and as if he was afraid of nothing. He looked like a warrior from another age. Fearless. Invincible.

Not the man in the barn who had looked

tormented with his desire for her, not the man with the angry words and proving himself infinitely capable of despatching that cool order to discard her from his life. He looked as if he absorbed everything that the world could hurl at him. Adversity was an empty word in his vocabulary. Her blood raced just to watch him move so easily with his mount. He still had the magic to excite her, despite everything that had happened.

They looked so good; the white tail streaming out behind the horse's gleaming flanks and the rider in the saddle so in command of his animal that he made it seem effortless, traversing in a gradual criss-cross pattern the rough land that sloped so deeply down on to the road. Unafraid of hidden rabbit holes, defying gravity, matching every pace with a careful eye and a steady hand on his rein, balancing himself perfectly in the saddle. Cool. The horse stumbled once, thrusting Joel forward, but she saw the gleam of his teeth, laughing, unfazed, not for a second showing alarm. He gave his mount time to balance herself, which she did, letting her gain her own confidence as she kept on going down, then they picked up speed as the incline lessened and he let the mare enjoy the gallop across the bottom of the field.

Instead of moving on she watched them until they had reached the edge of it where he leaned over and opened the gate that was set between the bulging growth of verdant hedgerow that bordered the fallow land and watched as he walked his mare through, deftly closing the gate behind them while still in the saddle. He began to walk her along the road in the direction of the village, his pace sedate, unruffled, a complete contrast now to the

burst of activity and energy as he had raced her
down the steep, roughened slopes.

Lucy turned the Renault back on to the track and
drove down to reach the road. Knowing she was
bound to overtake them made her feel on edge.
She followed them towards the village, aware of the
inevitable. Unfortunately as she approached horse
and rider she noticed a large milk lorry was slowly
advancing from the other direction and behind it
weaved a long tail of traffic. She groaned with
feeling. Joel glanced over his shoulder.

Lucy felt the knot of tension ball in her stomach.
She had no option but to drive slowly behind him.
The mare's tail swished and she danced sideways a
little, nervously flattening her ears with dislike at
the noise of the traffic and tossing her head a little
in protest. Joel soon had her strictly under control
and pressed on along the road, never looking back,
once he had established who was travelling slowly
behind him. He knew perfectly who it was.

That one dark look on his face had revealed it
when he glanced back. He was going to be difficult,
her face was set as she followed slowly behind
them, irritated beyond belief that he would not pull
his horse on to the grass verge to let her pass. It
would after all, have been much safer for him and
his horse as well as for passing vehicles. He was
making it as slow and difficult for her as he could.
He wanted her to feel uncomfortable, just as much
as he had humiliated her up on the fell in his barn.
She mentally squirmed at her undignified exit
from it. She wished she could hate him, she wanted
to – very much. He was making it extremely easy
for her to succumb to it.

The trail of oncoming traffic at last passed on

laboriously by and now that the road was clear she began to move her small car out to slowly overtake him, mindful of the quick, dancing nervous steps of his spirited mare as she started her manoeuvre. He had been waiting for it.

He rode his horse deliberately across the road, effectively blocking her way. She glared at him through the windscreen, wondering what game he was playing to attempt such a stupidly dangerous act. The mare's eyes rolled wildly, and her mouth worked at the bit, the metal parts of her tack jingling while her hooves moved restlessly on the road, the iron shoes ringing on its surface. Joel seemed to enjoy the perversity of their situation.

Lucy flung back her sunroof and stood up, peering out from the top of her car. 'What's the matter with you? I'd have thought you had more sense than to pull such a silly trick!'

'I want to talk to you.' The horse was still, suddenly calm. Now that his hand rested on her thickly muscled neck, she began to settle, and amazingly to Lucy stood perfectly still for him.

She studied his expressionless face and knew she could not bear another confrontation. 'You've said enough – and we've done enough – together in your barn, and I've nothing to say. Ride her past me, I want to get on.'

His mouth spread wryly. 'Moving out?'

'That's right – you'll be glad, I suppose.'

His brows darkened. 'I would like to think so – but you know that's not true.'

'Really?' she sneered. 'Don't pretend.'

Then he confused her. 'I want to apologize – about this morning. It wasn't fair, I want you to know that; I was angry, but that's no excuse to offer, but it's all I can say to justify what happened. Then there's the things I said to you.'

She thought about it and was not persuaded. This was his game. He liked hurting her, he was doing it all the time now. She could not forget what had happened. What he had said hurt, it still hurt, whether he considered them fair or not. 'You meant them, so – now I know – I have to go, anyway.'

'Going to London.'

'You've talked to Peter.'

'Hardly!'

'You don't like him. Why?'

'I neither like nor dislike him but I can hardly condone his leaving a young child without supervision in a strange place. Your attitude to being a family perplexes me.'

He had hit a target once again. Her eyes blazed and she snapped at him angrily, 'It's the way we are – and none of your business.'

The horse shook her mane and snorted, Joel looked rather amazed as he asked, 'Don't you mind?'

'Peter's free to live his life and I'm blowed if any man is going to dictate how I run mine. Look will you please move on – what if a car hurtles around at full speed?'

He looked at her impatiently, then carelessly remarked, 'I'll jump the hedge – if I'm pushed.'

'That's irresponsible!'

'Look who's talking!'

'What does it matter to you? We've said enough – don't you think?'

'The more you say the less I like it, Lucy.'

'That's your problem!'

'Is it? Don't you have a problem, Lucy, and doesn't it concern me or don't you give a care either way as long as you get what you want and hang anyone else?' He shook his head. 'I could never live easily with that philosophy.'

She stared at him, cold now with a fury that made her hands tremble on the wheel. How could he say those things? How could he be so unjust? She had not got what she wanted, had she?

'Get out of the way, Joel.' She sank down into the seat and began to move the car around them while keeping a wary eye on horse and rider. He looked very angry, his mouth a hard line, and his eyes were dark and bitter as she drove on until she was level with him.

He was shouting now, his voice stridently cold and bleak, as it rose above the sound of her engine. 'Is that all you really think about? Your career? Your own selfish needs?'

'Selfish! Don't use that word to me?' she shouted back, glaring at him while he stood his ground.

The look of contempt on his face was the last straw, her anger broke, she moved without thought, or care, stepping on the pedal and roaring away from him. In the rear mirror she saw the mare rear, her hind legs dancing with fright and attempting to regain her balance as Joel struggled to hold her. At the same time a rider on a high-powered motorbike suddenly, and it seemed out of nowhere, screamed past Lucy's car at some speed. She braked hard and because she was further out in the road than was necessary he had to swerve to avoid her, nearly ditching himself into the hedge but instead struggled with his bike until he almost spun round. She should have heard him coming, the bike was noisy enough now that it was upon them, but her anger had deflected her attention.

The biker glared at her from beneath his helmet, his mouth worked, shaping with colourful epithets, but he kept in his saddle and took off, right in front of Joel, his wheels screeching with power as he imitated the horse's movements in an ironic gesture, slamming back on to the road on both wheels and disappearing around the bend, the sound of his engine whining into the distance.

Lucy stared at Joel, whose attention was fixed on the terrified mare. She was trying to bolt, bucking and rearing while Lucy stared with horror as Joel fought to keep his seat and the mare under control, her shod hooves clattering now on to the road. Sweat glistened and frothed on her coat and saliva dripped from her mouth. Lucy felt fearfully helpless, wondering what she could do, while her hands shook with fright on the wheel.

She sat transfixed, watching him patiently master the mare with his hands and legs, while his mouth worked, talking to her continuously. Lucy's emotions seemed a strange mixture of gladness and dread, relieved he was not unseated yet terrified he might still get hurt. Even now, she could not deny how much that meant to her. The mare was quivering for action, Joel glanced across at Lucy, the look on his face hard and final. She saw him rein the mare's head to face the opposite gate across the road, he slapped her once, hard across the rump with the crop in his hand and she took off so quickly Lucy had to hold her breath as horse and rider, in one fluid movement, cleared the gate and disappeared into the field. His former words came back to her. 'If I'm pushed.' Well, he had jumped the gate. Was she pushing him out of her life now? Maybe that was right. Maybe the biker was a blessing in disguise. No one had been hurt. Not outwardly so.

He was riding out of her life and she knew he meant her to know it. He was master of his own actions again, firmly in control – the way he liked it. She looked ahead along the road, and without a backward glance drove her car forward with a similar disregard for reckless speed.

Ten

Sophia's train was late.

One hour overdue, Lucy noted anxiously glancing at the monitor on the station platform. She succumbed briefly to the agitation of it. Sophia was a niece not an offspring and, my goodness, had she found it a difference when explaining it to one's betters. Not that Madge was any better, far from it. She had her own problems, Lucy supposed, what with her married unemployable lover in Essex and her husband with the highly disposable income in Surrey along with their three teenage children siphoning off a large lump of it with their private education fees, but that was their affair. Madge Tremaine was diabolical – but she was her immediate boss.

She wondered how she had stuck it out working for her during the last few months but she had. Income demanded it. Fixed income that is, which paid the rent and the taxes. Flexibility was Lucy's favourite word these days. Not that Madge wanted to be. Still, she was grateful she supposed, that she had let her take the last hour off to meet the train, and then she had a whole week overseas before returning to work. She needed the break, the last three months had not been easy.

A railway official strode across the station concourse and Lucy made for him with some speed before anyone else could badger him for information. At least his news was more specific if hardly reassuring when she learned that a derailed goods train was fouling up the system. She resumed her seat on one of the benches and settled back with a resigned look on her face. Trade was building up she noted watching the influx of customers coming into the station from the nearby underground.

She could see directly outside into the street, through the wide glass doors, where taxis were pulling in with relentless monotony to drop off their fares. Her boredom was swiftly diverted when she recognized a famous politician, looking brisk and businesslike, carrying a bulging briefcase and a neatly folded *Evening Standard* tucked under his arm. He dashed through the doors and made his way, just in time, for the Edinburgh-bound InterCity was about to depart. Her eyes swung back to the cabs calling by outside, in the hope of spotting someone of equal interest, and she sucked in her breath with shock to watch Joel Mortimer pushing his way through the doors.

She slowly expelled her breath, aware of the pandemonium of heartbeats thumping beneath her rib-cage while her eyes absorbed every single detail, hungrily appraising his tall, virile appearance. Was he travelling home, she wondered, noting his lack of hand luggage, not even a sign of any ubiquitous brief-case? He wore no overcoat, despite the chilling onset of autumn, but his dark-blue wool worsted city suit was well tailored and smart, giving him the look of a man with means and substance, which he undoubtedly was,

and the crispness of his white shirt and light grey
tie looked freshly laundered.

Her heart lurched painfully. The pleasure of
seeing him after all these weeks demolished
without mercy the wall of protection she had
carefully nurtured. She was glad she was sitting
down, for she felt sure she would have been
staggering for composure otherwise. Her hands
gripped the edge of the bench while she watched
him stride with purpose across the concourse.

He looked thinner. Her eyes sharpened with
alarm. He had lost weight; there were hollows
accentuating his cheekbones, and his keen blue
eyes looked sad and shadowed. Perhaps he was
overworked? Strain etched sharply across his
features; he wore the look of a man burdened with
problems. He frowned at the monitor and glanced
at his wristwatch, his features taut with impatience.
His thick, short hair shone with health beneath the
station lights. Maybe he had a long wait too? He
was studying the group of people who were waiting
near the platform of an oncoming train, not that it
was the train she needed to jump up for, but it
afforded her the long, luxurious moment to let her
gaze feast greedily on him. The group of people
did not interest him for he turned away and began
searching the fairly packed concourse, distractedly
running his hand through his hair. He was looking
for somebody!

Lucy felt the sharpness of pain grip her insides.
Was it a woman, she wondered? His latest love?
Her thoughts began their study in torture yet she
was unable to tear her eyes away, wanting to notice
every beloved detail about him. She had missed
him so much, it was an undeniable fact. There had

never been a day during the last interminable months when he had not filled her mind. She recalled one weak moment when she had travelled across the city to seek out his chambers, turning away at the last moment before it was too late and so she had not made a complete love-sick fool of herself. Now, here he was, and watching him beginning to look rather frantically about him, she was afraid she was going to make a fool of herself all over again. He was definitely searching around for someone. Someone he knew. She closed her eyes, her mind seeing the vision of some beautifully glamorous woman emerging from the crowd, reaching out to be taken into his arms. How could she bear it, sitting here – waiting to watch the inevitable? When she opened them again he was staring straight at her.

She drew in a sharp breath, their eyes locking in one long poignant moment. She felt as if he had physically touched her. The strain eased from his face and he began to slowly walk in her direction, increasing her inner agitation. She was rooted with a numb shock, staring helplessly at him, unable to move, unable to flee, incapable of speech or direct thought. How many times had she yearned to see him again? Was she taking leave of her senses? Was all this a figment of her own tortured imagination? He was close now, getting closer. This was no dream. She glanced to either side of her. Her companions on the bench remained blissfully unaware of her inner consternation.

She was like a statue. Still. Silent. Wondering how she was going to handle this, unsure of what to do. The last time they had spoken was on the main road near his home, and while he struggled with his horse she was driving out of his life – or so she had thought. And so had he. Was he regretting his recognition of her? He looked far from pleased. His face was set and worried. The blood ebbed from her face and the ache in the pit of her stomach was real enough.

He was nearly upon her. She glanced sideways again, forcing herself out of her self-stricken immobility. The bench was full, two middle-aged women on one side, talking heatedly about train delays, and the remaining two occupants were men, travelling separately, engrossed in their evening papers. She stood up and with a nervous gesture hung the strap of her bag over her shoulder then advanced a few steps towards him.

She said the first thing that came into her head. 'Are you waiting for someone too?' Get it over with, her thoughts screamed inside her head.

'I've found her.' His eyes betrayed him, devouring her face with a need he could not disguise. 'How are you?'

Her pride got in the way. 'Oh! I'm fine,' she replied airily.

His brows met. 'The child's train is late?'

She looked around her before replying. 'You mean Sophia? How on earth did you know I was waiting for her?'

'A certain Madge Tremaine told me.'

'Madge? You've been talking to Madge. When?'

'Not long ago. I've spent some considerable time trying to find you – ringing every woman's publication throughout the country.'

Her face flared with heat. 'You've been looking for me?'

'Mrs Tremaine was very helpful – but more to

the point, I gather you're still living alone – in London.'

'I have a flat here—' Lucy explained slowly.

'She was helpful enough but understandably wary about giving me your address, and she would only tell me where you would be around this time. I came straight over.'

'It's half-term.'

'One of the obligations of being a parent – half-term beckons,' he commented. 'Is it your turn to have her come to stay?'

'Parent?'

'Well step-parent then,' he amended impatiently, 'the child told me about her real mother.'

'Step-parent?' she frowned, startled. 'Sorry, Joel – I don't know how or where you got that idea from.'

'What do you mean by that?'

'Sophia's my niece.'

'Niece!' He stared at her with a startled amazement.

'She's Peter's daughter.'

'Yes, I know she is.'

'And Peter's my brother – so that makes her my niece. Yes?'

He stared at her with a stunned expression washing over his face. 'Brother! He's your brother not your—' His thoughts troubled him for a moment. 'But you told Andrew Heskett he was your husband – you share the same name.'

'Why shouldn't I share the same name? I'm his adopted sister and I don't know what you're talking about. I've never said any rubbish about being his—' She groaned. 'Oh, I did! It was the day Winnie sent him down with some provisions and I thought he was a vagrant. I was scared and alone and pretended my husband was about. He must have thought—'

'So did I.' He ran his fingers through his gleaming hair. 'Even before Andrew mentioned his meeting with you.'

Lucy stared at him, speechless. She was trembling on the brink of the unknown. 'How could you make that assumption?'

'Sophia talked about you – the night I found the poor frightened mite wandering about outside the cottage. She was nervous about meeting her father's "very special person" whom he used to live with and who was travelling up to meet her – he wanted to surprise her when you arrived.'

'She thought I was a girl friend. I remember that!'

'Can you blame me thinking you were his estranged wife? A separation of three years – the cosy greeting in my damned kitchen. I was jealous then – sick with disappointment. You never explained—'

She was raising her voice, 'You never asked, you never told me—'

'I couldn't bear to say his name I was so jealous of him, and so guilty of wanting you. The child was so insecure – I felt I was breaking up your chances of reconciliation despite your declarations of being an independent woman. I couldn't see it that way. And so my guilt compounded.'

'So you sent me away.'

'As I saw the situation – yes! I had to!' he argued back with heat.

'Winnie knew the truth!' she cried.

'Oh, Lucy, come on, I could hardly bear my soul to my housekeeper.'

She felt foolish. 'I expect not.'

'Come on' – his hand reached for hers – 'let's find a less public spot to continue this,' he suggested, realizing the interest they were receiving from the packed bench behind her. Lucy glanced at the ladies, her heart hammering away at his startling revelation, grinning foolishly at the look of abject dismay on their faces that they were about to move away and rob them of an interesting episode. The men, po-faced, gazed down discreetly, seemingly glued to the headlines in their evening papers.

Joel spotted a couple about to vacate a secluded bench tucked away in a corner with a bank of plants conveniently arranged at one side that afforded its occupants some limited privacy. With his hand still enclosing hers they made their way to it. He glanced around impatiently as they sat down and faced each other.

'Just tell me, is there someone special in your life right now, Lucy?'

'Yes, there is as a matter of fact.' She saw the look of total dismay on his face, the misery that clouded his piercing blue eyes. 'I'm looking at him.'

His eyes were serious. 'I want to share my life with you; I want to put right everything between us; I have so much to give you.'

'I only want you, Joel. I love you.'

She felt his fingers gently on her hair, brushing back the copper tangle of curls. 'I treated you so badly, yet even then I couldn't stop myself falling in love with you – lying to you to make you go away. I thought I'd get over you—'

She caught his fingers against her cheek with her hand and brushed her mouth against his palm. 'You were terribly cruel.'

His voice harshened. 'Did you think it was easy for me to tell you to go? I couldn't stand it. I missed you so much, ached for you, until I could bear it no longer. I had to know if you and he were still apart. It's been three months, I thought if you were still alone then I couldn't be the reason for your failed relationship and I needed to know if you still wanted me. I was going quietly out of my head thinking about you so much. By Manny's records, all I had to go on was a Stateside address – his address. I could hardly contact your brother for your forwarding address when I understood him to be your estranged husband.'

Her eyes widened. 'So you found me through Madge. That's amusing. She's not keen on me.'

'I'm keen.' His rich voice was warm with feeling, and he pressed closer towards her. 'I've made some incredibly silly mistakes. Maybe if my temper had not sent me directly back to Cap Ferrat that night – the night you left – then I might have sorted the whole thing out with your brother and we needn't have wasted three long, empty, wasted months.'

She was trembling again. The ache a real knot of need inside her. 'And now?' she asked him, her mouth dry.

His gaze was hungry. 'Nothing's changed,' he said simply. 'I still love you very much.' He lowered his head towards her and covered her eager mouth with his own. There was a commotion on the other side of the plants. They both drew away, and the moment was lost. A group of young men strolled up, laden with luggage. It prompted Lucy to check her watch. 'We'll have to go – Sophia and the others – the train might be in already. They'll be frantic.'

'The others?'

'Oh, the Pallisters from Glenridding have been staying with relations near Sophia's school. They're accompanying her up to London and then – well, I'll explain later.'

His mind was bent on other things, but he stood up with an obvious reluctance to do so, his hand at her elbow. 'Come on then,' he sighed, 'I guess our business will have to wait.'

They hurried across the packed station concourse together, and made straight for the platform just as the express was pulling in. He stood behind her, his arms possessively clasped around her shoulders. Lucy was breathless with happiness. His breath teased her ear. 'There's just one thing—'

Her heart seemed to somersault and she turned around at the concern in his voice, but he was smiling, and her fears receded for his eyes were warm and full of love. 'One thing?' she queried, fascinated by the sensual curve of his mouth, which seemed to be getting closer and closer to her own as his hold tightened more effectively around her.

'You won't mind if I arrange the marriage – our marriage. The sooner I can get my wedding ring on your finger, Lucy Elliot, the better I'll sleep at night.'

'Oh darling.'

'You will marry me, as soon as I can decently arrange it?'

Her cheeks glowed with delight. 'Indecent haste would suit me fine.'

He laughed softly. 'I love you very much.'

She smiled. 'And I love you, madly, distractedly, wonderfully!' She grimaced. 'I have a very tiny flat

– and guests staying tonight.' She did not tell him about her plans for tomorrow or the fact that she had every intention of cancelling them. There were other things to share and discuss yet.

'Our first minor problem. Will your brother be there? I suppose I'll have to break the news to him. He'll be thrilled,' Joel muttered wryly.

'He's still in the States but you're going to have to get used to him, after all you'll be brothers-in-law.'

He looked towards the platform and sighed cheerfully. 'It's a small sacrifice.'

Lucy did not care. Peter would be jealous too – at first, but then, she knew her brother had very serious things on his mind these days, judging by his letters, and very soon, Lucy was going to have to take third place in his heart.

She watched the train come in slowly, aware of the pressure of Joel's hands on her shoulders, turning her slowly towards him. People streamed from the opening doors of the carriages. A child sprang down on to the platform and looked along it, past the passengers blocking her view, and glimpsed a sight of them first, before the others. She giggled with excitement as her young friend jumped down to join her. 'Look Caroline, I can see Lucy – who's that man? He's giving her a huge kiss. Look, they don't care who's looking at them!'

Caroline giggled and looked up at her mother. Susan Pallister was too immersed in withdrawing their considerable luggage to notice at first, but when she did, and recognized them, she could not stem her surprise or her smile. As she began to walk with the children, who helped with the baggage, down the platform towards the still oblivious couple she felt convinced Lucy was not with them on the New York flight in the morning after all. Peter would be disappointed, she supposed, but the fact did not worry her. She would just have to make up for it. The thought filled her with satisfaction.

Lucy sighed against the comfort of his embrace. 'I'm afraid we're not going to get much time alone.'

He smoothed the soft skin of her cheek with one hand. 'You can stay with me tonight. I have a small service flat in Park Lane, didn't I mention it? I'm sure Susan Pallister can cope with the children at your place.'

'But we must meet them in the morning to see them off at Heathrow.'

'I'll personally wake you.' His eyes were lazy, thinking about it.

'I'll look forward to that,' she whispered back.

His hand lingered on Lucy's cheek, his thumb traced her upper lip. Her tremulous mouth waited, soft and inviting, and the look in her eyes touched a cord inside him. He wanted to crush her to him again and never let her go. He wanted to do a lot more than that and her body quivered beneath his hands as he took her by the shoulders and pressed her to him. He wanted to think of nothing else at the moment.

People smiled as they passed by. He grinned back at them. His world was no longer grey, nor would it ever be, he thought with the deep conviction within his heart, as long as he had her by his side, and he let Lucy know it – in front of them all.